Beyond Reach of the Law

By G. H. Teed

From the **Union Jack** Magazine,
Series 2, No. 485, 25 January 1913.

Stillwoods Edition, 2019

Stillwoods.Blogspot.Ca

Catalogue Information:
Title: Beyond Reach of the Law
By G. H. Teed (1886-1938)
First published: The Union Jack magazine, Series 2, No. 485, 25 January 1913.
This Edition by: Stillwoods, 2019. (Doug Frizzle)
ISBN Canada: 978-1-988304-94-6
Blog: Stillwoods.Blogspot.Ca
Author Blog: http://ghteed.blogspot.com/
Storefront: http://www.lulu.com/spotlight/lulubook22

This story appeared later as **The Girl Who Made Pearls** in Detective Weekly magazine, No. 351, 11 Nov. 1939.
Keywords: Sexton Blake, British fictional detective, Yvonne Cartier.

The Skipper desires to draw his readers' attention to the fact that "Beyond Reach of the Law" has been written expressly for this issue of the Union Jack.
Introducing the Great Princess of Mystery.
For Readers of All Ages –of Either Sex.
No. 1 of Our Great New Series of Stories.
A Yarn with an Interest All Its Own.
Yvonne v. Sexton Blake.

Stillwoods Editions are a poor complement to some great stories and authors. Doug Frizzle is 'Stillwoods'; in retirement I needed something to do on 'foul weather' days.

First I found the author, A. Hyatt Verrill, from New Haven, Conn. He had been prolific and popular in his time but was forgotten even to Wikipedia. His books were difficult to locate—they were acquired from used book dealers as far away as Australia and South Africa. They were such great reading I began to republish them. I started with an autobiography of the author, unpublished, that I located at University of British Columbia—that Archive had no idea how they acquired it!

So I entered the publishing business. I am using Lulu.Com; it is a print on demand publisher so the costs are quite manageable. I spent

15 years on Verrill!

Then I found 'Luke Allan', a Canadian, namely, Lacey Amy, who wrote stories while he travelled the world, but they were mostly about 'Blue Pete' an American Half-breed who evades his enemies by going to Canada; Medicine Hat, Alberta, to be exact, and is befriended by a Mountie. Again these books were scarce, and no one knew this author was a Canadian. There are Stillwoods Editions of all of his 54 novels—two were published anonymously!

Lately, I've discovered New Brunswick's G. H. Teed, 1886-1938—prolific and forgotten. The vast majority of his 400+ novels were published anonymously and as 'pulp' novels. They were available weekly on England's newsstands and were very popular but as they were made of inferior paper, they deteriorated quickly. But over the years, English collectors speculated and researched these works, discovering a series of authors, and G. H. Teed was one of the greatest!

Teed's works were mystery and suspense—detective novels featuring 'Sexton Blake' or 'Nelson Lee' as cerebral sleuths with great physical training. As this 'About Stillwoods' is being created, one collector of Sexton Blake has provided me with some 200 scans of Teed novels. At this time I have re-published about 65 of his works as either blog posts, or, the longer stories as Lulu imprints.

So that is the story on Stillwoods and myself, there are a few other authors and works I have added along in my journeys.

The quality of Stillwoods Editions is perhaps not great. I have no training in any of this digitizing and publishing business. I do not stop to make perfect products. I would rather have ten ones, than one ten!

I hope you enjoy these authors—their works are nearly a hundred years old!

Thanks to the author and collector, Mark Hodder, many of the Sexton Blake stories by G. H. Teed stories have been made available to Stillwoods Publisher. Many thanks to Mark!!!

Disclaimer: Each work may contain language and racial terms that is not appropriate to today. I apologize for them; I know that the author was using his voice to excite an adventurous English audience. Most every work has characters of redeeming ethnicity within.

I hope you enjoy and share these stories; I have.

Doug Frizzle

frizzle@hfx.eastlink.ca

About G. H. Teed

There are discrepancies in the reports on the history of G. H. Teed. This narrative is mine and may be more or less accurate.

George Heber Teed was born 1886 near Saint Stephen, New Brunswick, Canada. His father was a landowner and entrepreneur. He was educated in New Brunswick and then was sent to McGill University, where he probably graduated about 1907.

He had an itch for travel and for the Caribbean; once the travel bug got him he travelled far. He worked in Costa Rica and Australia before he travelled to England and began to write detective thrillers.

He was not great with money, he was very social and spent much time in taverns. Reports are that he was often in debt even though he was a prolific writer in popular magazines.

He took some time off in war service in the Great War.

He spent considerable time in France.

He also took a few years off around 1921, again getting the travel bug. These travels were around the world. These travels added authenticity to his stories, and his stories always had excellent plots and characters.

He died in 1938. Some of his works are listed as by G. Hamilton Teed—apparently he did not like Heber, so he adopted Hamilton as a familiar name.

Perhaps the best description of the man and his works is contained in the book 'Forgotten Authors Volume 3' by Steve Holland.

G. H. Teed books available at:

http://www.lulu.com/spotlight/lulubook22

Bottom of Suez
Crooks' Vendetta
Voodoo Island
Five in Fear
The Grey Ghost
The Case of the Duplicate Key
The Temple of Many Visions

Gangland's Decree
The Clue of the Four Wigs
The Mystery of the Film City
The Black Abbot
Murder Ship
Spies Ltd.
A Mystery of the Big Woods
The Mystery of the Kidnapped Killer
The Secret of the Swamp
The Case of the Pink Macaw
The Terror of Gold-digger Creek
The Case of the Mummified Hand
Pearls of Doom
The Victim of the Gang
The Case of the Courtlandt Jewels
Nelson Lee and the Lhassa Red Menace
The Riddle of the Russian Gold
Voodoo Vengeance
Hounded Down
Bribery and Corruption
The Sacred Sphere
The Tiger of Canton
The Crook of Marsden Manor
The Affair of the Six Ikons
The Secret of the Coconut Groves
The Case of the Disguised Apache
Under the Eagle's Wing
The Rogues' Republic
The Mitcham Murder Mystery
The Brotherhood of the Yellow Beetle
When Greek Meets Greek
Bootleg Island
The Broken Span

See http://ghteed.blogspot.com/
For some of G. H. Teed's shorter works and articles about this
Canadian author.

PROLOGUE.   I.   The Great Mining Swindle.

THE afternoon sun was dipping behind the hills of an Australian mining camp.

Silhouetted against the deep-blue sky were the derricks of the mines which lined the ridge, looking frail and flimsy in the distance. The cable wheels still spun round on most of them, bringing up rich loads of quartz to be swallowed by the smelter.

The line of mines followed the visible outcrop, stretching away in the distance, and against the tool house of one in particular—the Jig Saw—leaned two men.

They were both bearded but while one was dressed with immaculate care, the other bore marks of toil, and his garments were rough. An intimacy evidently existed between them, for they spoke in confidential tones, and looked warily around from time to time.

"I'll tell you, Pearson, now is the time," the city man was saying. "If we bring it to a head while they are out here, we can get things wound up at once. On the other hand, if we wait until they return to England—well, it means correspondence, and we don't want any more of that than is necessary in a deal of this kind."

"Maybe you're right, Ike," responded the man called Pearson. "What do the others say?"

"They're all agreed. I tell you, Jim, now is the time."

"All right, if all of you think so, I'm agreeable; but I would have liked another three months to get the stone out of this saddle formation. The gold is fairly sticking out of it, and if anyone got down on that level they'd twig in a minute."

"Oh, Mrs. Cartier won't send anyone down! She doesn't know anything about mines or business, and the girl knows less. Things will go beautifully. You'll see. I'm no fool at money juggling," Ike grinned. "And when Ike Vineburg takes on a thing it usually goes through. This means a cool million amongst the eight of us, and, from what you say, the mine ought to show another."

"It'll do that all right," grunted Pearson. "I've been in a good many mining districts—from Alaska to Chile—but this beats any prospect I've ever tackled. It's simply reeking with the stuff!"

Vineburg's eyes glittered with greed as he listened, and his tongue moistened his lips with anticipation.

"I'll go ahead with the deal," he said briskly. "You know, your part. Don't on any account let anyone you don't trust down the mine."

"Leave that to me. I didn't go in on this without careful consideration, and I'm taking no chances. When do you start to knock the price down?"

"I'll get things going to-morrow," answered Vineburg. "The others will start dumping their shares on the market in big blocks, and I'll circulate the report that the mine has petered out. People will come up to you, as the manager, and ask for a confirmation of the news. You tell them the yarn we arranged, and that means in twenty-four hours all the small holders will rush to sell. I will buy every share up quietly as it comes on the market, and when the bottom has dropped out, I will wire Mrs. Cartier to run down from the station."

"Do you think she will turn over the station as security to float a loan?"

"Of course. Before Cartier died he told her the Jig Saw was the richest thing in sight, and when I tell her we simply must borrow to carry on further working, and provide new machinery, she will bite beautifully. You leave that to me. I can handle her; she's as simple as a baby, and will do just what I say."

"It seems to me it'll be risky transferring to ourselves the shares and deeds of the station afterwards," remarked Pearson, dubiously.

"I've arranged for that. I'll provide dummies to loan us the money on the deeds, and when the further work fails, we will tell her the mine has snuffed out entirely. All she can do is to swallow the medicine. As we will apparently be heavy losers as well, she won't suspect anything. Ten to one she'll go back to England at once, and then we can make the transfer back to ourselves."

"I guess you've got a shrewder brain than I have," said Pearson, with an admiring glance. "I couldn't have engineered a deal like that in a thousand years."

"I haven't been a bookmaker for twenty years for nothing," laughed Vineburg, in a self-satisfied manner.

"By the way, Ike," went on Pearson, "what's going to win the cup this year? Anything strong favourite yet?"

"Tragedy Prince," came the prompt reply. "Put your socks and boots on it—it can't lose. And I don't tell you that because I own him, neither. He's the best piece of horseflesh in Australia to-day."

"I guess I'll leave it alone," grinned Pearson. "I don't think I'll risk much with you on the betting game, Ike. It's poor business, judging from the thousands Cartier lost with you."

"Cartier was an easy mark," replied the bookmaker, with a contemptuous snap of the fingers. "He'd trust anybody. As for me, I wouldn't take my own brother's word, on oath, on the race track."

"I don't blame you, Ike," returned the other, acidly. "I've heard it wasn't worth much."

"I didn't speak literally!" snapped Vineburg, flushing. "But take the tip, or leave it. I wouldn't take your money on Tragedy Prince in any event. I'm putting a fortune on him myself."

"All right, Ike," smiled Pearson, good humouredly. "Don't lose your temper. If you back him yourself, maybe, I'll put a couple of thousand on him, But about this other matter. Will you start smashing the price to-morrow?"

"Yes," replied Vineburg, in a modified tone, "I'll get along now, and tip off the boys. Have your story ready, Jim. And, for Heaven's sake, don't let anything leak out from this end!"

"I tell you I can trust every man I've got!" snapped Pearson impatiently. "You handle your end, and I'll guarantee nothing leaks out here."

"Very well. I'll slip up again in a week or so, and let you know how things go."

"Right!"

A few-seconds later Vineburg was scrambling down the side of the hill to a buggy which waited below, and Pearson turned away to enter his rude quarters.

．　　　．　　　．　　　．

The day following the conversation between Pearson and Vineburg was a memorable one on the small mining exchange, which transacted business in the shares of the surrounding mines.

Soon after it had opened for the day's business, disturbing rumours crept about that all was not well with the Jig Saw. The famous saddle formation from which the mine had secured so much gold, and the discovery of which had boomed the price of the shares, was reported to have petered out. Later rumours seemed to confirm this, and further details gave a minute description of how shafts had been driven in all directions to try and pick up the "legs" again, but that they had ended in nothing.

The price of the shares had dropped, and fluctuated unsteadily at the first report; but later news had sent them down helter-skelter.

They firmed a bit when Todd and Kelly—two of the biggest stockholders, appeared on the floor, for it was reported that they had come to deny the rumours. But when, instead, they threw large blocks of shares on the market, the smaller holders, who had been hanging on desperately waiting for official news, lost their nerve, and rushed to sell.

Several brokers were buying up the shares at bargain prices; but where they could afford to hold for the reaction, the small holders could not.

Men had rushed off to the mine to ask the manager if the report was true, and when they returned and fought madly for a sale, the panic grew general.

Early in the morning the price had stood at nearly five pounds per share, but on the close of business they were offered at five shillings, and holders were hopeless of receiving even that. Further selling orders had come in from Melbourne, Sydney, and Adelaide on the news which had been telegraphed to these centres, and the outlook for the next day was black.

The worst anticipations were realised, for further large blocks were thrown on the market wholesale, and on the evening of the second day Jig Saw shares stood at two and six, which meant no value.

On the same evening a lady stepped from the train at the little station. She was small, and delicate-looking, and dressed in mourning. A heavy, black veil obscured her features; but as she raised it to greet a man who came up to her, the light from the platform lamp shone on a sweet, gentle face, which must have been very beautiful in its youth.

"Ah, Mrs. Cartier," exclaimed the man effusively, "I trust your journey hasn't been very tiresome?"

"How do you do, Mr. Vineburg?" she replied, in a clear, sweet voice. "No; I was too worried to notice the discomfort. I came immediately on getting your telegram. Are things any better to-day?" she asked anxiously.

"I'm sorry to say, Mrs. Cartier, that they are much worse," answered Vineburg, in a gloomy tone. "I have done all I could to stem the tide; but my pocket has a bottom, and I had to give it up. I hardly dare reckon my losses."

"But is the report true, Mr. Vineburg, that there is no more gold in the mine?"

"I'm afraid it is, Mrs. Cartier. It is a big blow to us all, and I regret exceedingly that your husband is not alive. I had great faith in the Jig Saw; and we might save things yet, if he were here."

"Save things! How do you mean, Mr. Vineburg?" she asked eagerly. "I know my husband had every confidence in the mine. I don't know anything but what you tell me about such things; but if it is anything I can do, let me know what it is. I know Mr. Cartier would do almost anything to save the Jig Saw."

Vineburg's eyes gleamed as she spoke; but they assumed a sorrowful expression as he turned to answer.

"I'm afraid you don't understand, Mrs. Cartier. You see," he went on, as one speaking to a child, "there is only one direction left in which we can drive to try to pick up the vein. It will take a great deal of money, and the credit of the mine is gone now. I would gladly put up all I have, but I have already done so, and the other directors have done the same. We would need to borrow a great deal of money to go ahead. Mr. Cartier would have saved the situation; but I am afraid we must swallow the loss." And he sighed admirably.

"I am afraid I'm very stupid, Mr. Vineburg. Tell me what would Mr. Cartier have done?"

They had been walking down the main street as they talked, and had arrived at the entrance of the hotel. The light from its entrance shone across the footpath, and Vineburg stopped in the shadow to reply.

"Well," he laughed, "it won't do any good to tell you; but I feel sure he would have arranged the loan for us by putting up the necessary security."

"Security!" she echoed. "What security?"

"He had such perfect faith in the mine that I feel positive he would even have temporarily pledged his station—temporarily, you understand."

He gazed beneath lowered lids as she gasped:

"But, Mr. Vineburg, that is all I have left now, since the shares have gone. Do you think he would have pledged it?"

He nodded, without speaking, for he knew the value of silence at such a time.

"I'll—I'll think over it to-night, Mr. Vineburg, and let you know in the morning. Good-night! Are you sure my husband would have done that, Mr. Vineburg?" she turned back to ask. "If he would—

5

why, I suppose I ought to as well."

Again he bowed silently, and then, bidding her goodnight, hastened down the street. As he turned the corner a triumphant smile flitted across his face, for he know she would do it.

Ike Vineburg had not been a bookmaker for twenty years without knowing the tricks of the game and the gullibility of human nature.

Yvonne in her native element.

TINKER GASPED IN ASTONISHMENT AS HE SAW THE BEAUTIFUL WOMAN WHO ENTERED

II. Bad News.

IT was six months after the panic in Jig Saw shares.

Binabong Station preened itself proudly in the warm rays of the sun.

Its fertile acres, freshly green from the tender shoots of young grass, stretched for miles in every direction.

The giant trees threw their welcome shadow at intervals, and here and there a large clump had been left where the ground was swampy.

The house was a low, rambling structure, covered with vines, and its corrugated roof threw back the suns rays with a trying glare. Canvas curtains shut in the verandah from the persevering rays, and several sheep dogs lay listlessly in the shade.

The surrounding garden was, however, unaffected, for its stalks were still vigorous with the life of spring.

To the left of the homestead was the horse paddock, while in the rear stretched a vivid patch of lucerne, forming a foreground for the anxiously cared-for field of ambercane, which would make rich fattening food for the aged ewes in the summer when the grass was sparse and dry. From the right came the refreshing murmur of a huge overshot dam, fed by the towering pillar of the artesian spring. Shearing was in progress, and from the sheds came the steady hum of the machines as the heavy fleeces dropped to the floor. Stretched, over the home paddock were hundreds of newly-shorn sheep, looking ridiculously naked, while from the yards surrounding the sheds came the mournful bleat of those still waiting their turn. The sharp bark of a dog sounded, accompanied by the shrill cries of the stockmen as they drove some of the waiting sheep into the pens as a finished mob poured out at the other end.

Inside the shed all was bustle. Men, stripped to singlet and trousers, sweated over sheep which lay helpless between their knees. Occasionally the blade would go deeper than intended, and a red patch would appear, vivid against the new whiteness. A loud call of "tar" brought the tar boy on the run, and the red patch was soon changed to black by the application of the brush.

Other men rapidly gathered up the fleeces as they fell to the floor from the last snap of the shears, and threw them dexterously on the large tables, where others quickly "skirted" them around the edges, the fleeces going into their proper piles according to class, and the

8

skirtings going to swell the rapidly increasing pile of "locks," "bellies," or "pieces," as the case might be.

Further on, the wool-press rapidly pressed the finished fleeces into large bales, which a boy branded as the pressman finished sewing and released them.

A slow moving team of bullocks loaded up as the completed bale was rolled aside, removing them to a high-floored shed where they were safe from the dampness.

Half a mile away, in a large paddock, a traction-engine "chugged, chugged," followed by two large disc ploughs. Behind came a fine-cutting disc harrows, and sharp diamond-tooth harrows brought up the procession, for the overseer of Binabong believed in fallowing, and fallowing well.

Riding a big chestnut with the grace of the born stockman, was a slim, bronze-haired girl. A broad-brimmed felt hat sat carelessly on her head, and the neat, divided skirt dropped in straight lines to the small feet booted in heavy tan. Her face was flushed with a warm colour, and her lips were parted in a happy, unconscious smile as she cracked a long stock whip, and sent a shaggy sheep dog flying around the mob of ewes which she was mustering.

To the casual observer the scene on Binabong Station that beautiful day presented an ideal picture of industry, peace, and prosperity, with consequent happiness. No cloud, either figurative or literal, obscured the horizon, but a tiny speck which appeared in the distance, and which rapidly grew larger as it approached, was to obscure the happy scene with a startling swiftness.

As it grew more distinct it resolved itself into a horse and jinker, in which were seated two dusty men. The driver turned toward the house as they reached the home paddock, and the jinker rattled over the soft turf, to the accompaniment of the fierce barking of the dogs which, tired from mustering, rested in the shade of the verandah.

As the sound of the dogs reached her ears, the girl lifted her head, and, shading her eyes, looked intently in the direction of the house. A puzzled line appeared between her deep, serious eyes, and she turned with a sharp exclamation to the boundary rider who accompanied her.

"Strangers, Jerry. I'll have to go to the house. Take over the mob, and keep the dog."

"All right, Miss Cartier," replied the tanned stockman and, winding up her stock-whip, she rode at a clinking pace for the house.

The strangers had already disappeared through the wire door when she arrived, and, tossing the bridle rein to a black boy, she hastened in after them, for she imagined her mother would be asleep, and there would be no one to welcome the new-comers.

She was right, for the visitors sat alone in the cool gloom of a wicker furnished reception-room, wiping their wet foreheads.

They rose, and bowed, as she entered.

"I'm sorry," she began. "I saw you arrive, and came as quickly as possible. Did you wish to see my mother? She usually rests in the afternoon."

"It is our turn to apologise—Miss Cartier, I presume," replied the darker of the two; and, as she nodded, he went on: "We are sorry to disturb Mrs. Cartier, but the maid insisted on calling her. We could have waited until her usual time for appearing. Besides, this room is delightful after the sun." And his teeth flashed as he smiled at her.

"But allow us to introduce ourselves. My companion, Mr. Morgan—Miss Carrier. My name is Vineburg," he added, with another flash of the white teeth.

The girl bowed, and replied:

"Mother wouldn't mind being roused, but she has been ill lately, and I am very anxious about her. However, I expect she'll be here presently, and if you'll excuse me I'll order some refreshment for you. It is hot in the sun."

They bowed their thanks, and resumed their seats as she left.

"By Jove, Morgan, isn't she a stunner!" whispered Vineburg. "Did you ever see such hair?"

"Oh, you're caught by every pretty face!" growled Morgan. "Now, I—" But he broke off as Mrs. Cartier entered.

She looked pale and tired, and held out her hand to Vineburg with a listless gesture.

"This is a surprise, Mr. Vineburg," she smiled; "but, nevertheless, you are welcome."

"Thank you, Mrs. Cartier," returned Vineburg suavely. "Believe me, madam, I would not have come if it hadn't been urgent. But permit me to introduce Mr. Morgan. You have heard me speak of him as one of the directors of the Jig Saw." he explained, as Mrs. Cartier acknowledged the introduction.

"Yes, I remember," she murmured, as she sank into a chair; "but you speak of urgent business, Mr. Vineburg. I trust you have no further bad news about the mine?"

The conversation was interrupted by the entrance of Miss Cartier, accompanied by a maid carrying a tea-tray. General topics were discussed while the travellers refreshed themselves, and presently Miss Cartier rose to leave, but her mother put out her hand.

"Don't go, Yvonne! It is business about the mine."

"All right, mother dear," replied Yvonne, resuming her seat. "But are you well enough to talk business this afternoon? Can't it wait?"

"No, dear. Mr. Vineburg says it is urgent, and now, if you don't mind," she added, turning to Vineburg, who seemed the spokesman of the pair, "please let me hear what it is?"

"Well," answered Vineburg hesitatingly "you must prepare yourself for bad news, Mrs. Cartier. The fact, is—er—"

"Go on, please!" cried Mrs. Cartier, in an anxious tone. "Don't keep me in suspense! Have we lost more money?"

"Yes, that is the case," replied Vineburg hurriedly, as though anxious to get the words out. "We've lost a lot; in fact, Mrs. Cartier, the Jig Saw mine is a total failure."

Yvonne jumped up and rushed to her mother's side. She was only twenty-three, but she could see tragedy in the eyes which she held so dear, and the protective instinct, which she had inherited from her father, quickly asserted itself. She passed her arm around her mother's shoulder, and turned toward the men to speak, but Mrs. Cartier gathered her strength together to reply.

"And that means?" she whispered.

Vineburg's eyes fell before her terror-stricken gaze, and Morgan shifted uneasily in his seat.

"It means," replied Vineburg, clearing his throat, "that the collateral must be forfeited to the creditors. They are clamouring for their money."

"I—I think I understand, Mr. Vineburg," faltered the stricken woman. "It means Binabong must go?"

Her eyes dwelt with a despairing intensity on his face, and as he bowed his head in silent assent, she dropped to the floor with a low moan. Both men jumped to their feet as she did so, but Yvonne waved them back. Picking the frail body up in her strong young arms, she stumbled from the room, her eyes blinded with tears, and went down the corridor to her mother's chamber. Tenderly she laid her on the bed, and hastily sponged the hot temples,

"By Jove!" muttered Morgan. "I've got enough decency left in me to be disgusted with myself for being in this!"

"Oh, shut up!" replied Vineburg. "We've started on it, and it must go through. If you are so squeamish you should have said so." But he held his eyes averted as he spoke.

Inside the chamber, Yvonne worked feverishly. She finally heaved a sigh of relief as the unconscious woman's eyes opened.

"Oh, mother, mother dear, don't take it so hard! It won't make any difference to us. We'll go back to England, and be happy there again. Don't—please don't worry about it, dear!"

Her mother's eyes stared straight ahead, and Yvonne's filled with an unknown terror as she saw the lips moving, but knew they were not speaking to her. She bent her head to listen, the tears falling thickly on the coverlet.

The sick woman seemed unaware of the girl's presence, and seemed to be addressing someone else.

"Forgive me John!" she whispered. "I did it because I thought you would have me do it. The mine was dear to you, and that made it dear to me. You told me, John, to be careful.

"Oh, Yvonne!" she wailed, turning to the girl. "Your father suspected before he died that he was being swindled, and he took measures to protect us, and now when it is too late I see it all. Those two villains and their confederates have deliberately ruined us! They have everything! And now—now, my poor child, we are penniless! Oh, Yvonne, my dear daughter, what will become of you, all alone and penniless, amongst—"

But the frail body gave way under the strain, and the weary spirit fled.

It had only kept on under protest ever since John Cartier had died, and since then its only tie with earth had been its passionate love for Yvonne, for she typified in a feminine degree all the self-reliant virtues of her father.

The mother dropped back before Yvonne was aware what had happened. She gazed in horror for a moment, then feverishly she called into the deaf ears, and madly she pleaded with the still lips to speak.

She pressed her head to the shrunken breast, but no throb sounded from the still heart, and as she lifted her head, she realised for the first time the awful truth.

Her eyes hardened, and, turning, she staggered from the room and up the corridor to where the visitors sat.

They stared in amazement at the wild look in her eyes, and started to speak, but she silenced them with an imperious gesture. Her voice came with a strange, husky sound, but cleared as she went on. She spoke slowly and emphatically, and her words fell like icy drops in that dim room.

"I am unaware," she said, "of the exact details as to how you have succeeded in your dastardly and cowardly purpose! I knew when my mother came back from her trip to the mine, and said she had turned over the station to you as security for a loan, that you were taking advantage of her ignorance of business matters! But now I know that you swindled my father, and that he suspected you, and that you have deliberately swindled my poor mother and myself out of everything we had! If the law will reach you, rest assured it shall! But I imagine you have been clever enough to carry out your dastardly schemes within the fringe of the law! First you cheated us out of the mine, and now out of our home!

"For the money or the station I don't care; but my dear mother."—and her voice broke pitifully for a moment— "lies dead—dead—do you understand?—in the next room, and you your dastardly schemes have killed her! Hear me now, and mark well what I say! I swear I will never rest until I have caused each and everyone of you to suffer as you have made her suffer! Don't say to yourself that it is the raving of a grief-stricken girl—it isn't! Now go! Go quickly, before I call the dogs to drive you from the place! In a week's time you may send your jackals to take possession of the station!"

All Vineburg's suave confidence had departed under the stinging lash of her words, and, picking up his hat, he slunk through the door with Morgan following.

When the sound of their steps died away, Yvonne turned and went back to the still figure in that other room. As her eyes fell on the cold, stiff features, her tense body relaxed; she staggered weakly to the bed. and fell prostrate across her mother's body in a raging torrent of grief.

.　　.　　.　　.

Yvonne found, on going through her mother's papers after the funeral, that, there was no doubt about the swindle.

Her shrewd young mind read between the lines what her mother had failed to see, and when she left the station at the end of the week, penniless and alone, her heart was filled with bitter anger against the men who had ruined them.

She laid the case before a lawyer in Melbourne, but after going into it he shook his head.

"It's no use, Miss Cartier," he said. "There isn't the slightest doubt but that you and your mother were swindled out of the mine and the station, but they have done it too cleverly for the law to reach them.

"That is the fault of the law, and the innocent must suffer. It is unfortunate that such is the case, but we cannot alter it."

Yvonne rose wearily and passed out. As she gained the street, heedless of the passers-by, she raised her hand, and said:

"I swear I will not rest until I have tracked down and ruined everyone who had a part in our mine!"

III.   Vineburg Takes on a New Hand.

"IKE" VINEBURG, bookmaker and owner of many racehorses, was in good humour as he walked into his training-stables, one clear, bright morning shortly after his rather undignified departure from Binabong Station.

From his own point of view he had reason to be, for the previous afternoon had seen the end of the business connected with the transfer of the station and the Jig Saw mine back to its old owners.

In a few months, when things had blown over a bit, they could announce another rich discovery of gold, and the shares would boom. And in the meantime—well, the station was showing a big profit under the new management, and his "book" had been doing particularly well of late.

His horses had also won several minor races; and Tragedy Prince, the apple of his eye, was shaping even better than he had dared to hope, and if it continued to show such form, it looked certain that his colours would be carried to victory in the Melbourne Cup in November. He flushed as he remembered his last visit to the station.

Heavens, she did go off pop, but her words were only the ravings of a girl. Besides, she had left the station a month previously, and he had heard nothing of her since. Chances were, she had returned to England. "She'd cool off a bit when she got down to pounding a typewriter for a living." And he grinned, for the picture pleased his fancy.

He greeted Lee, his trainer, with particular affability, and astonished that worthy man by offering him a cigar. For Ike Vineburg had never been known to give away very much.

"How is Tragedy Prince this morning?" he asked.

"Splendid, sir!" answered Lee. "If he keeps like he is now, there's no question about the Cup!"

"Good! Don't let him get stale, Lee."

"Indeed I won't, Mr. Vineburg!" responded the trainer. "I'm out to get the Cup for you this year, and we've got the horse that can do it."

"By the way," went on Vineburg, "have you succeeded in getting anybody interested in Firefly?"

"No, sir; and I'm sorry. His reputation as a vicious horse is too well known. It's a pity, too. He's only eating his head off here since

15

they brought him from the tracks."

"H'm! Well, let's have a look at him. I feel pretty fit this morning, and if he doesn't look too vicious, I'll try him around the stable-paddock for a bit."

"I would advise you not to, Mr. Vineburg," remarked Lee. "He'll kill you, or try to, anyway!"

"Oh, I'm not afraid of him!" laughed Vineburg. "I'm no dab in the saddle. Thrash him into submission. That's my motto."

The trainer reluctantly led the way to a stall where a black gelding stood. It had for some time been barred from the racecourse on account of its vicious habits at the barrier, and as the trainer approached, it lashed out savagely.

"Saddle him up, Lee," said Vineburg. "I'll try him."

Lee knew from experience that argument was useless. Picking up a saddle and bridle, and watching his chance, he dashed in beside the gelding; he succeeded in putting them on, and backed the horse out. The two men led it through the stable to the rear, where the trainer held it for Vineburg to mount.

As the bookmaker did so, a slim, red-headed boy appeared from round the corner of the stable and stood watching the performance. It would have been hard to recognise in the ragged boy, the girl who, only a month before, had been the happy Yvonne, but such it was. Her disguise was perfect, and her natural slimness assisted her immensely.

Vineburg started around the paddock, but before he had covered a hundred yards the gelding began to show temper.

Vineburg may have found his motto, "Thrash him into submission" a successful one with men, but when he applied it to the black gelding that morning he made a mistake. He brought his whip down with a vicious cut as the horse showed its temper. It was like a match to a cask of gunpowder. The gelding reared on its hind legs, its mouth opening viciously as it felt the sting of the whip.

Vineburg held his seat, but when the horse dropped back, and, turning, bit savagely at his leg, he lost his nerve. When again it reared he clawed madly for a moment at its neck, and then rolled with a cry from its back.

The gelding dropped to the ground, and leaped forward, and Lee gave a gasp of horror as he saw one of Vineburg's feet still sticking in the stirrup. Those flashing, plunging hoofs would surely beat his brains out!

The trainer dashed forward in an endeavour to catch the maddened animal; but as he did so, a slim figure passed him. It was the ragged boy who had been watching the performance, and Lee stopped in amazement as he watched the lad.

Over the turf bounded the boy, and as the horse and fallen rider approached, he watched his chance.

Springing, not for the horse's head, but for its back, he succeeded in clutching the saddle. The horse shied wildly and bit at him, but the boy held on; evading the snapping teeth, he vaulted with all his strength, and, although the horse again plunged, the boy landed safely. He grasped the bridle-reins, and the battle began.

Every moment it looked as though the horse would bring its feet down on the head of the now unconscious Vineburg, but the boy with marvellous skill kept it clear. While he kept the horse busy, the trainer, who had followed, dragged Vineburg free.

It is needless to go into the details of the battle which followed. It was fierce and desperate, and many times in a half-hour, which seemed like an eternity, the boy barely saved himself from falling beneath the plunging hoofs.

Vineburg had recovered, and as the boy pulled up the conquered horse, he approached and held out his hand, but the boy did not seem to see it, for his own remained occupied with the horse. Vineburg unsuspiciously pulled his back, and spoke.

"You have saved my life, my lad, and I wish to thank you."

"Oh, that's all right, sir!" answered the boy.

"You don't look too prosperous," continued Vineburg: "and if you will come into the stable, I will see what I can do for you. By the way, you can ride all right. How would you like a job here?"

"I'd like it first rate, sir. I came to see if you needed a boy."

"Well, that's fortunate! What weight are you?"

"About eight stone, sir."

"And your name?"

"Tom, sir,"

"Tom what?"

"Just Tom, nothing else."

"H'm! Yes—well, you'll have to take a second one to ride under. Now, go along with Mr. Lee and get fixed up."

Again thanking the boy, he turned on his heel to go and change his mud-stained clothes.

He would have been a very astounded man had he seen the veiled look which followed him, for he would have seen a great resemblance to a look he had received from an angry girl at Binabong. But, unfortunately for him, he didn't know, Yvonne followed the trainer to her new quarters.

That look of Yvonne's had been an expression of her intention. On leaving the lawyer's she had racked her brains in an endeavour to devise some form of revenge against the men who had ruined her home. Vineburg was close at hand, and her funds were low, consequently she decided to start on him first.

Again she racked her brains for a scheme to follow, and there it was that her magnificent gift of riding aided her. Her plans once formed, she had quickly put them into effect, and luck had favoured her, for now she had the position she desired in the very stable of her enemy.

"You can bunk in here, Tom," said the trainer, throwing open a small door which led into a dark box of a room. "If you're hungry, go up to the house and get something."

"Thank you, sir," Replied Tom; and such was Yvonne's entrance, as the jockey Tom, into the stable of Ike Vineburg.

Vineburg was right when he said Tom could ride.

The new jockey got his first mount at an important meeting at Aspendale, and got home an easy winner. A string of successes at Sandown, Williamstown, Moornee Valley, and Caulfield tracks followed, and Tom's "percentages" having been carefully saved he now had a snug account in the bank.

It was after a specially brilliant win at Caulfield that Vineburg came to him and promised him the mount on Tragedy Prince, for the rapidly-approaching Melbourne Cup.

Cup Day dawned warm and sunny.

Business in Melbourne was practically suspended for the day, and the streets swarmed with visitors from every part of the Commonwealth, as well as a fair number from England, for the Melbourne Cup is world famous.

By midday a steady stream started in the direction of Flemington, where the race is run, and by half-past one the beautiful course presented a lively appearance.

The crowd was enormous—well over a hundred thousand people.

On the lawn were congregated a dazzling array of feminine beauty, vying with each other in the advantageous display of beautiful and expensive gowns.

Beyond, under the trees in the betting-ring, the strident tones of the bookmakers were just starting to call the odds, and still further on a steady stream poured into the bird-cage to gaze on the horses which were being either led about, or carefully attended, in preparation for the coming events.

The jockeys scattered about lent a tinge of colour to the scene, and many an anxious-faced punter hovered near, waiting for a word which would send him scuttling away to put his money on.

Behind the main grand stand on the hill, the more moderate-priced crowd thronged as densely, and the steady stream of arriving flat patrons straggled out for half a mile or more.

But whether in the paddock, the hill, or the flat, the ever-present tipster rushed about, recklessly dealing out valuable information on sure things and moral certainties which the owner, a close friend (?) of his, had told him as a special favour. Such was Flemington on "Cup Day."

As the betting settled down, and particular horses were mentioned, Tragedy Prince was made a strong favourite.

Vineburg had not adopted any secrecy, for as soon as the betting opened he had sent his men through the ring, placing his money in all directions. The result was that the Prince soon firmed from the nominal opening price of eights down to threes.

The Viennese, who had shown great promise in Sydney had opened at almost the same price as Tragedy Prince; but as the money came in thousands for the stallion, she drifted to twenties, Trafalgar, the idol of the people, shortened in price, coming to the multitudinous small bets of the general public, and remained firm at sixes. Aurifodina came next at sevens, and the rest of the numerous field trailed along until, any price was offered against some.

The first two races had been run, and the weighing-out bell for the Cup had rung, when a sudden stir occurred in the betting-ring. Punters, who had held their money until the last thing, hurried after several rushing figures which had invaded the ring to listen to their bets. A gasp of amazement went up as thousands were laid on The Viennese as the emissaries were known agents of the stable, a general rush took place to get on; and the mare shortened quickly to fives, and then, when still more money came, she went to fours. Tragedy Prince eased a point, and when the horses went to the barrier, both the mare and the stallion went out equal favourites.

Only three people on the course knew the real reason for the sudden popularity of The Viennese—two were the owner and the trainer, and the other was Tom Fair (Yvonne had taken the name Fair to ride under), who was riding the other favourite, and real choice of the punters, Tragedy Prince.

That reason had emanated from a private conversation which Tom had had the preceding evening with Morrison, the owner of The Viennese. Tom had sounded the owner carefully, and, the latter, guessing at the lad's meaning had arranged an interview. There he put the question plainly to Tom. Would he pull up Tragedy Prince, and permit The Viennese to win over him? Tom had passed his word, and Morrison was a very astounded man when Tom refused any money for doing so.

Morrison naturally became suspicious that a double game of some sort was on, for he had been prepared to go as high as a thousand for a guarantee that Tragedy Prince would be "dead"; but his suspicions were quickly allayed when Tom, who had come prepared, passed over to Morrison every penny he had saved, which amounted to a very respectable sum, with the percentages he had won in minor races.

Morrison took the money, and promised to put it on The Viennese at the longest price possible, and, consequently, he had waited confidently during the betting until his horse drifted to twenties before he made a single bet.

The barrier flew up, and the horses got away fairly well together. Roseboy, a stable mate of Tragedy Prince, took the lead, setting the pace for the field. Auriodina was second and Trafalgar third, Tragedy Prince fourth, and The Viennese fifth. From that on, the field bunched in twos and threes, the unreliable Caro bringing up the rear.

In this order they passed the stand, accompanied by the excited urgings of their backers, and from the "flat" Trafalgar's name predominated, showing the shillings and half-crowns of the patrons there had evidently gone on the old favourite.

As the string pulled around to the back, Roseboy dropped out, and Aurifodina took the lead. Trafalgar shortly went back to fourth place, and, on passing the Abbattoirs, The Viennese came with a fine spurt, and secured a lead of nearly a length.

The excitement was intense. A momentary hush fell as the horses swept into the straight, and a deafening chorus of yells and hysterical feminine shrieks greeted the oncoming animals.

"Tragedy Prince—Tragedy Prince! He'll do it! No! It's The Viennese! Come on, Trafalgar! Tragedy Prince! Look at him coming up on the outside! He'll do it yet! Wake him up Fair! Give him the whip! The Viennese— The Viennese!"

On swept the horses, The Viennese still holding the lead, Trafalgar next, and Tragedy Prince coming up rapidly on the outside. Tom brought him on with a sudden slash of the whip. The stallion leaped forward, and, as they went past the judge, he seemed to have won it by a nose from The Viennese, with Trafalgar third. But Tom knew he had just lost. He was too good a horseman to have left his spurt even that fraction of a second too late, if he wanted to win. And when the numbers went up giving the race to The Viennese, with Tragedy Prince second, a mingling of groans and cheers went up from the spectators, according to whether they were on the winner or not.

Probably not one rider in a hundred could have made such a show of trying to win, and intentionally lose by as close a margin as had Tom. But he had calculated to a nicety, and when the numbers went up not one of the eagle-eyed stewards knew that Tragedy Prince, in being placed second, was placed just exactly where his rider had intended him to be placed.

Tom had a strenuous half-hour with the disappointed and angry Vineburg at the stable that night, and in the early dawn he faded away as mysteriously as he came.

A run of luck as a punter increased his already large banking account to a very substantial sum, and three months later Yvonne sailed for Europe.

Mr. Ike Vineburg was mystified on receiving a note, couched in the following terms:

"A very small credit has been placed to your account. The balance of the account will be collected at another time.—YVONNE CARTIER."

Vineburg knit his brows in an ugly frown as he read the note; but his temper had not been of the best since he lost the cup, and he tore it up in a rage, cursing the girl for trying to play some practical joke upon him.

It never occurred to him to connect his former rider, Tom, with the writer of that note.

IV. The Compact.

THE tropical sun blazed down with a fierce intensity. The sea rolled in oily laziness, while the surf flung itself in a never-ending rainbow-coloured assault over the coral reef of the little South Sea Island.

Inside, a deep-hued lagoon lapped against the beach; the cocoanut-palms and banana-trees forming a vivid background to the attractive picture.

Riding gracefully at anchor in the lagoon lay a rakish, white yacht, with the speedy cut of a racehorse, her shining brass catching the sun, and throwing it back in dazzling streaks. White-garbed sailors worked busily about her deck, endeavouring to find a soiled spot on her already spotless paint.

A large awning was stretched across the stern, and in its cool shade a beautiful, bronze-haired girl stretched gracefully in a wicker deck-chair. Beside her, on a small wicker stand, was a long glass of lemon, in which the ice still clinked, and face down in her lap lay a large volume.

Reclining opposite was a middle-aged man in white flannels. He had just been speaking, and wore a cynical smile as he awaited her reply.

"Yes, I'm quite ready to descend upon society, as you put it, Uncle Jack. When mother was stricken down by the machinations of those scoundrels I vowed vengeance, because I felt they had robbed her.

"Possibly I would have been satisfied with my youthful revenge on Vineburg at the Cup; but, afterwards, as you know, I found those papers amongst my father's belongings, which really pointed to Vineburg and his crowd as a gang of clever rascals. Since then, as you know, I have toiled almost night and day for revenge, and six years of preparations have left me as resolved as ever."

"Yes, I understand," drawled the man. "But why not do as I suggest? You've got the brains and the shrewdness, and together we can make a nice thing out of society. Personally, I've got to do something, for, to be frank, I'm stony. I admire the success of rascals like Vineburg, but loathe their methods; but with forethought we can work in perfect safety, particularly if you bring into use some of the latest scientific discoveries which you say you are able to apply."

"Well, uncle, I'm almost inclined to agree with you. Every man on the yacht is safe, for they have been chosen for that purpose, and, as you know, Captain Vaughan lost his ship, and was unjustly blamed. He is quite prepared to wage a war upon society. But if I agree to extend my ideas from the men I had in mind to society in general, it will be on a strictly business basis. It must be clearly understood that I am the sole head, and that my word is law. Moreover, that none of the circle make any attempts of any kind without submitting them to me, and that everything is to be planned and executed according to my ideas. If you think you can live up to that—well, we will talk it over to-night with Captain Vaughan and Hendricks, the mate."

The eyes of Graves, her uncle, gleamed with satisfaction as Yvonne spoke, and he rose with a sigh of relief.

"Good girl! I can see my troubles are at an end. Au revoir until dinner!" And the wayward brother of Yvonne's gentle mother went below humming gaily to himself.

Yvonne remained alone, gazing in brooding silence over the tropical sea.

Beyond, through the trees which lined the lagoon, appeared a solitary light from the luxurious retreat which, the far-seeing Yvonne had built for herself in case of need.

The boy came to announce dinner, and, with a heavy sigh, the girl rose, and descended the companionway. On reaching the lower-deck, she bent her footsteps towards the after part.

Yvonne passed through the saloon and followed a short passage which opened into a broader one stretching the whole width of the yacht. She pulled a tiny brass key from a chain round her neck and opened a door, turning a switch as she did so.

The light revealed a large saloon covered with a thick carpet, on which her feet made no sound as she carefully closed the door and moved across the room.

The sloping sides of the yacht each formed a wall, which was covered with books. Opposite the door, and stretching from side to side, was ranged the most complete laboratory equipment the most exacting professor could wish. Strange brass and steel instruments of every conceivable shape and size filled every available space in the room, and over the long, glass-covered work table were hundreds of bottles and test-tubes, containing mysterious powders and liquids.

Overhead was a maze of different sized wires—some as large as one's little finger, and some as delicate as a thread.

Yvonne glanced lovingly about as she moved to a small crucible in which was a greenish-coloured liquid. She carefully poured in a few drops of another liquid, and returned to the door.

Again looking about her, she paused before opening the door, and her lips moved.

"At last—at last! Six years of studying, working day and night. But I can move at last. Vineburg first, then the other seven."

Her eyes hardened, and her hands clenched as she spoke the words to a whisper. Turning slowly, she switched out the light, and passed out, emerging a moment later with a smile into the brilliantly-lighted saloon, where the gleaming silver twinkled against the snowy table linen, and the delicately-upholstered furniture contrasted with a pleasing dignity against the cedar and black palm woodwork.

End of the Prologue.

"IT'S certainly a magnificent affair, but I'm afraid it's I more than I wish to pay."

The speaker was a tall, middle-aged man, immaculately dressed, and his words were addressed to Bechstein, the proprietor of the famous Bond Street jewellery establishment.

They stood near the window in the latter's private room, examining a beautiful string of pearls which the customer held in his right hand. From his left dangled a walking-stick with a gold filigree handle, and he swung it carelessly to and fro as he made the remark.

Bechstein rubbed his hands, and smiled in an insinuating manner. The customer's demand to see a finer assortment of pearls than were displayed in the outer shop had brought the proprietor himself hurrying to handle the fastidious customer, and they had gone into the private room, where the jeweller pulled forth several exquisite strings from his private safe.

"It is a fair price, but not too much for the stones, sir," he replied. "See the exquisite colouring, the unrivalled purity; it is impossible to match it in Europe. And fifty thousand—it is money, yes, but the pearls! Ah, sir, they have not their equals! But what was that?" he broke off to inquire. "Ah, yes, the sunlight on the gold of your stick. I saw the flash, but did not notice the stick before. But, as I was saying, sir, these gems are second to none."

"I know—I know," replied the other, laying them back in the tray with a sigh. "But it is a lot of money. However, I will think it over, Mr. Bechstein, and let you know. By the way, I will leave you my card."

"Thank you, Mr."—the jeweller paused as he read the name engraved on the card— "Mr. Morris. I will be pleased to do anything I can to suit you; but hadn't you better reconsider your decision? Say forty-eight thousand cash— that's as much as I could really afford to take off."

"No, I won't decide to-day," said Morris, turning towards the door. "I'll be in again in any event, and if I purchase at all will do so here."

"I'm sure that is very kind of you, Mr. Morris," remarked the suave Bechstein, as he bowed his guest out to the accompaniment of much hand washing. "It will be a great pleasure to me." And he again smiled with oily politeness as the customer nodded and departed.

Bechstein returned to the tray of gems as the door closed, and, after glancing with genuine admiration at the beautiful string which had been the subject of the conversation, he carefully locked them away.

"He'll come back," he muttered. "He's dead taken with it, and means to have it. Probably didn't intend to go so high, and wants to realise on some securities. But it's worth the money. It's the finest thing I've seen in the five years I've been here. Nice mess, the countess going bankrupt and leaving it on my hands. I'll have to do something with it soon; can't afford to let that amount be idle in the safe."

He moved toward the door, grumbling to himself, but on emerging into the outer-shop his suave smile returned as he went forward to greet more customers.

Some days passed, and in the press of business the jeweller had given little thought to the man who had admired the large necklace. But he had need of a large sum in a few days, and as he sat in his office one foggy afternoon planning ways and means, his mind reverted to Morris.

"Never came back," he muttered, "I should have persuaded him to pay a deposit. He's probably cooled off, and decided the price was too stiff. Wonder who he was, anyway? Talked a bit like an American. However, I've got to have money by the first of the week, and I don't see anything for it but to get the bank to loan me on the pearls. I hate to do it, but—"

His musings were interrupted by a knock at the door, which opened to admit a lady, followed by an assistant.

"This lady desires to see something in necklaces, more valuable than we have outside, sir, so I thought you would desire to show her some yourself," said the assistant.

"Certainly—certainly!" smiled Bechstein, rising. "'Won't you be seated, madam, and I will show you some very fine gems."

"Thank you!" replied the lady, in a low, sweet voice, lifting her veil as the assistant retired.

Bechstein's observant gaze saw a beautiful face, surmounted by deep, serious eyes, and beneath the broad hat was visible distracting waves of gleaming bronze hair. Her garb was simple in the extreme, but the jeweller was judge enough to know that it was from an exclusive and expensive establishment. He glowed with satisfaction as his quick eyes noted the fact, for the suave Hebrew liked dealing with wealthy ladies. He had an almost uncanny knowledge of their weaknesses, and he played on the strings of their vibrations with the skill of a great musician.

He opened the safe, and drew out a tray of glittering gems, in the centre of which reposed, like a queen surrounded by her women, the magnificent necklace of pearls. He knew the value of first impressions, and cleverly placed the tray so that the light fell at just the right angle on the stones, throwing into bold relief the central string.

The fair customer gasped as she saw the fascinating display, and the jeweller dropped his eyes to hide his satisfaction as her hand involuntarily went out and was quickly withdrawn.

"They are exquisite—exquisite!" she murmured rapturously. "That beautiful one in the centre; it is perfect! Don't touch it, I beg of you!" she cried, as the jeweller reached for it. "Let me admire it for a moment first. The light falls so perfectly on it."

Bechstein had quickly pulled back as she spoke, cursing himself for being too precipitous. She was evidently a finer-tuned instrument than the average feminine customer, and would need delicate handling. But he smiled inwardly with satisfaction, for her every detail breathed affluence, and he considered a sale as good as made.

"Oh, how lovely!" she breathed again, putting forth her hand, and this time picking up the gems. "But I suppose it is very expensive?" And she looked inquiringly at the jeweller.

"It is listed at sixty thousand, madam," replied Bechstein, "but for an immediate sale, I would let you have it at almost cost—say fifty thousand net. It was made for the Countess of Brent, but was left on my hands. Every stone is a picked one; it hasn't its equal for beauty and purity."

"Yes—yes, it is exquisite; but the price is far, far more than I can pay. I only wish for something moderate."

She laid it down with a sigh, and picked up a smaller string.

"How much is this one, please?"

Bechstein was disappointed, but he concealed his chagrin, and smiled in his usual manner as he replied. He had not yet lost hope.

"That, of course, is much smaller, but I can guarantee every stone to be absolutely perfect. It is worth four thousand."

"I am sorry you showed me the large one now," she said, with a silvery laugh. "This is nearer the price I wished to pay."

Fifteen minutes were spent in examining the other contents of the tray, but at the end of that time the customer returned to the smaller of the pearl necklaces.

"I think I'll decide on this one," she said. "If you will make it thirty-five hundred I will take it with me. The other is far beyond my means."

"It is impossible to take off that much, madam, but I will make it thirty-seven fifty. I am sorry you won't consider the large one. It is an unparalleled opportunity."

"Perhaps I will return with my uncle in a few days, and try to persuade him to buy it. A thing like that is just the same as saving the money, isn't it?" she asked innocently. "However, I will leave it to-day, and take the other."

"Any bank would be glad to loan a good sum on the large one," replied the jeweller. "I would suggest you brought your uncle in as you mention. I am sure he would endorse my statements."

"I am sure he would," she murmured, as Bechstein turned to get a case for the small string which she had purchased.

She counted out the notes, and a few moments later rose to depart with her purchase in her bag, the jeweller deferentially accompanying her to the street entrance.

He bowed low as she climbed into a large red motor, and almost forgot his poise in astonishment as she entered the driver's seat and took the wheel, the car having no chauffeur.

"It's a pity," remarked the jeweller to himself, he hastened back to his private room to put away the gems, which he had for the moment forgotten.

"I'll give her three days to come back, but I'm afraid she won't. If she had intended taking the big one, she wouldn't have bought the small one. If I don't sell it in three days, I'll have to borrow on it, that's all."

He had reached his private room, and heaved a sigh of relief as he saw the gems were just as he had left them. It was careless of him, as customers in the outer shop were near the door of the private room.

He locked them away, and sat down once more to figure ways and means.

For five years had Bechstein been the proprietor of the jewellery establishment in Bond Street. That he had borne the name Vineburg in Australia, was known only to himself. A hasty departure had made it impossible to realise on as much as he might, had he had more time at his disposal. On his arrival in 'Frisco, he had taken the name of Bechstein, and arriving in London a short time later, had taken up his old profession of dealing in precious stones.

Every available penny had gone to purchase the Bond Street business, and trade having been bad the past few months, he had been financing himself by strenuous measures.

The throwing back on his hands of the expensive necklace, which had made a heavy drain on his available funds, had been a tremendous blow, and his financial condition presented a gloomy aspect at the present moment.

As the jeweller feared, the fair customer did not return, and four days later he placed the necklace carefully in his pocket and left the shop.

He would go to Isaacs first. Isaacs was a large diamond merchant and knew the value of stones. He would probably loan more on the pearls than would the bank. He hailed a taxi, and twenty minutes later sat in the private office of the busy diamond merchant.

Bechstein wasted no time in preliminaries, and rapidly stated his request.

"Thertainly, thertainly, my friend," repeated Isaacs, with a strong Hebrew accent. "Have you the stones with you?"

"Yes," answered Bechstein, pulling out a velvet case and opening it. "The finest lot I've ever seen."

Isaacs took it from him, and looked at it with admiration.

"Beautiful! Beautiful, Bechstein! Vonderful purity! Vonderful colouring!"

He turned and placed them on the desk in front of him, picking up a glass as he did so.

"Just a formality," he laughed apologetically, as he bent to examine them, and Bechstein smiled serenely, knowing the value of the great string.

"Isaacs must be a careful customer," he decided, with an inward grin. "He takes long enough to test them."

"Are you frightened they are false?" he said aloud, in a joking manner. "Here! What—" he began, half rising, as Isaacs deliberately picked up a small hammer and cracked lightly at each pearl.

Bechstein's eyes widened in speechless horror as each pearl broke, and a thin covering fell off, leaving nothing but a common glass centre.

Isaac's jaw set grimly, and his eyes glittered angrily, as he gathered up the pieces and passed them back.

"Is this a practical joke, Mr. Bechstein?" he said icily. "If so, I must say it is in exceedingly bad taste!"

"Good heavens! You don't think I knew they were false, do you?" almost screamed Bechstein frantically. "I swear to you I don't understand it! I got them specially from Craig's for the Countess of Brent, and they haven't been out of the shop since!"

"I believe you, Mr. Bechstein. You have evidently been the victim of a very clever fraud. They are the finest imitations I have ever theen. If it hadn't been for a tiny crack in one of them, I vould have passed them as genuine. I vould advise you to put the police on the matter at vunce."

Bechstein sat in a huddled heap. His voice had deserted him, the sweat stood in great beads on his forehead, and his eyes stared in fascinated horror at the pieces of the necklace in his hand.

"No, not the police!" he moaned. "Keep it quiet, Isaacs! I have heavy payments coming on, and if this got out my credit would be ruined! What will I do—what will I do? Fifty thousand pounds!"

The mention of the money caused a fresh convulsion of his features. He jumped to his feet, muttering incoherently as he jammed his hat on his head and dashed wildly out the door, clutching in his hand the broken pearls.

Isaacs turned back to his desk with a shake of the head.

"Poor Bechstein!" he murmured. "I'm afraid he'll never trace the man that did that job!"

BECHSTEIN entered his private room and locked the door. Sinking into a chair, he dropped his head on the desk. His brain was in a whirl, and his reasoning power was stunned by the shock of the discovery.

"Good heavens!" he whispered. "Fifty thousand pounds just when things are critical!"

He crouched motionless, heedless of the passage of time. The assistants had come from time to time and knocked timidly on the door, but the jeweller paid no attention, and they went away, not daring to knock again.

Hours passed and still he sat motionless, and not until night closed down did he move. He stumbled wearily to his feet and smoothed his hair. Gathering himself together he unlocked the door and entered the outer shop, where the assistants were packing away the trays of jewellery preparatory to leaving for the night.

The head assistant came up, and Bechstein spoke, his voice husky in spite of himself.

"I haven't been very well this afternoon, Ford. Anything of importance?"

"No, sir," replied the assistant. "I knocked once or twice, but as you didn't answer I thought you must be feeling unwell. Can I do anything, sir?"

"No, thank you, Ford. It's only a bad headache. I've got some writing to do, and will remain for a while. Just put the spring-lock on when you go."

"Very good, sir." And as the assistant hastened away, Bechstein returned to the private room.

"It's a mystery to me," he muttered, dropping wearily into his chair again. "Only Ford has a duplicate key of this safe, and he is absolutely beyond suspicion. I've only had it out three times—once when I showed it to Sir George Wellington, once when that American Morris was here, and again when I sold the small necklace to that woman three days ago. It hasn't been out of my sight for a moment, and— But hold on, I did leave it for a few moments when I went out with the lady to the street; but it couldn't have happened then."

He picked up the pieces of the imitation and looked closely at them.

"Perfect in every detail, even the filigree work on the clasp is exact; and the stones themselves, they're marvellous! No, it didn't happen then! The person who made this imitation would need detailed drawings to scale to execute the work. It's uncanny, even the small bend which the original had in its clasp has been reproduced. Is it possible it has been done while it lay at Craig's, and that they have been duped?"

A gleam of hope lit up his eyes for a moment, but despair soon succeeded again. "No hope there!" he muttered. "But the question is—what am I going to do? If I put it in the hands of the police it will get out, and with things in such a critical condition it would send me to the wall.

"No, that won't do. If I only knew—ah! Wonder if I could get that chap Blake? They say he is a marvel! I'll look him up in the 'phone book and see if he is on the line."

He found Sexton Blake's number, and made the call, being answered by a clear, boyish voice.

"Is that Mr. Blake's residence?" inquired the jeweller.

"Yes. Who is speaking, please?" came the reply.

"Bechstein, the Bond Street jeweller. This isn't Mr. Blake speaking, is it?"

"No, sir. I am Tinker, his assistant. But I'll call the guv'nor. Just hold the line, please."

Bechstein waited impatiently for some moments until a deep, distinct voice came over the wire.

"Yes. Mr. Bechstein, this is Sexton Blake. What can I for you?"

"Are you very busy, Mr. Blake?"

"Well, yes, I am rather. Is it anything important?"

"It is of the utmost urgency. A very serious thing has happened, and I would like your advice. I would go up to your residence, but perhaps you would prefer to come here where I could better explain?"

"I can spare an hour or so, and will come straight along," replied the famous detective; and Bechstein felt a little less hopeless as he hung up the receiver.

"From what I've heard he can ferret the thing out if anyone can," he muttered, pacing the floor restlessly as he waited Blake's arrival.

He hastened quickly to the door as the detective rattled it and led the way to the private room.

"Now, Mr. Bechstein," began Blake briskly, "just what is the trouble?"

He dropped into a chair with his back to the light, and faced the jeweller, who walked up and down nervously.

"The trouble is, Mr. Blake, that I've been robbed of a fifty-thousand pound string of pearls, and if I don't get it back quick, I'll go to the wall with a ruined credit!"

Blake's eyebrows went up almost imperceptibly.

"That is certainly a serious loss, Mr. Bechstein. Supposing you give me the facts, and then I will let you know if I can spare the time to take the case. Firstly though—have you informed the police?"

"No!" replied the jeweller heavily. "That would mean publicity and consequent ruin, which I'm trying to avoid."

"I see," nodded Blake. "Well, what are the facts?"

"As far as I can see, Mr. Blake, there are no facts." jerked out the jeweller.

"Keep yourself in hand, Mr. Bechstein," said Blake, seeing the jeweller was labouring under strong emotion. "You say you have been robbed. That in itself is a fact, consequently there must be other details."

The jeweller collected himself a little under the influence of the calm voice of the detective.

"I'll tell you all I know myself!" he cried desperately. "But I can't see for the life of me where you will find anything to help you solve it. Some weeks ago I ordered Craig's, the big importers, to pick up a number of the choicest pearls for me which they could find. Three weeks later they sent word that they had secured the number I needed. I took a run down to their place, and was very pleased with the selection. A few days later they delivered it, and I put it in the safe. I had got it for a special order for the Countess of Brent; but, as you know, she lost everything through the failure of Green & Co., and it was left on my hands. Since then I have only had it out on three occasions—one to show it to Sir George Wallington, the second time to show it to an American by the name of Morris, and the third time when I sold a cheaper string to a lady."

"What was the lady's name?" asked Blake abruptly.

"The receipt was made out in the name of Miss Cole. Here is the imitation," went on the jeweller, handing the pieces to Blake, who thrust them carelessly on one side.

"I never dreamed there was anything wrong until I took the one you see to Isaacs, the diamond merchant. As I told you, I am temporarily in need of funds, and intended borrowing from Isaacs, giving the necklace as security. He examined it, and discovered by a tiny mark on one of the pearls that the whole thing was false, otherwise, it would have passed the keenest judge. It is the most perfect imitation I ever saw. Every detail is exactly like the original— this filigree clasp, this bend in it, the chain, everything. That is the story, Mr. Blake."

The great detective had sat motionless as the jeweller told his story. From outside appearances he seemed to take no interest in the narrative; for he had thrust the necklace aside when Bechstein passed it to him, and he had not even glanced around as the jeweller pointed out the similarity in the workmanship. Only a tense look in the eyes indicated that the brilliant mind was working with lightning-like rapidity— every word the jeweller said being either tossed aside as useless, or carefully stowed away for future investigation. Rapidly the keen reasoning power started on the construction of the circle, and if the jeweller didn't see the meaning of the questions which Blake rapidly asked, it mattered not to the great detective.

"Now, Mr. Bechstein, listen carefully, please! We will start at the beginning, and please answer my questions as clearly as possible."

"Very well, Mr. Blake, I will do my best," replied Bechstein, sinking wearily into a chair. "Go ahead!"

"We will eliminate Craig's for the moment," continued Blake. "There is, of course, the possibility that the substitution might have happened there, and I will look into that point later. Now, to start from the day you received it from them, and placed it in your safe. Firstly, has anyone else a key of the safe besides yourself?"

"Yes, Ford, my chief assistant; but he is beyond suspicion, Mr. Blake. Besides, it would take hours to make the detailed sketches according to scale, and no one else had the opportunity. I am here all day nearly, and a watchman has been on at night ever since the robbery in Regent Street, two months ago."

"You say you showed the pearls first to Sir George Wallington?" went on Blake.

"Yes."

"How long had you had them here when that occurred?"

"Nearly a week."

"Where were you at the time?"

"Right here. He sat where I am, and I lifted the tray out, and laid it on the desk in front of where you are sitting."

"How long was he here?" asked Blake.

"Not over five minutes altogether."

"You noticed nothing at all out of the ordinary?"

"Yes. He just remarked that it was a deuced fine thing, and, after admiring it a bit, laid it back on the tray. I immediately put them back, and we went out together."

"How long after did this American—Morris—look at them?"

"About ten days."·

"Was it in here also?"

"Yes. He sat at first in the same chair in which Sir George had sat; but when I passed him the necklace, we walked over to the window."

"Did you notice anything at all out of the ordinary while he was here?"

"No, nothing. I do remember remarking once about the sun reflecting from the gold on the end of the handle of his stick; but I don't suppose you mean trifles like that."

"Nothing is a trifle in a matter of this kind, Mr. Bechstein," remarked Blake quietly. "Did you have your eye on the pearls all the time he was here?"

"Yes, every second. I'm very careful that way. I'm positive on that point. He didn't stay more than a few minutes either."

"And you say the next time was when you took it out to show a lady—a Miss Cole?"

"Yes."

"She bought a small string?"

"Yes; and paid cash for it."

"How much did it come to?"

"It was four thousand, and I let her have it for thirty-seven-fifty cash."

"Anything out of the ordinary with her?"

"No. She admired the big string, as women will, but put it down. She looked over everything in the tray, but, finally decided to take the small one."

"Did you lose sight of it at all?"

"I did for about two seconds; but the necklace was in exactly the same position when I turned back. Even if she had been able to substitute, I would have heard her movements. And besides, how could she have an imitation? It would take hours to sketch it, let alone the days of expert work afterwards."

"Did she stay long?" went on the detective.

"No, not long. I went to the door with her. She got into a big, red car, which she drove herself. The few minutes I spent in going to the door with her was the only period in which the necklace was out of my sight. I had neglected to put them back; but everything was undisturbed when I returned, and I wasn't more than three minutes altogether."

"Where was Ford when you returned—do you remember?"

"Yes. He was serving a lady out near the door. It would have been impossible for him to get in here and back in the time."

The great detective did not reply; but sat buried in deep thought for some time. Bechstein watched him anxiously, hope and despair alternately chasing themselves across his face. He jumped nervously as Blake suddenly broke the silence.

"I will take the case, Mr. Bechstein. It presents some most unusual features, and, at the present moment, nothing is very clear. But I will go ahead on it at once."

"Thank you, Mr. Blake!" replied Bechstein, his voice husky with relief. "It means failure to me if you don't succeed; but I know if anyone can, you can."

"I will do my best," answered Blake. "By the way, is Ford, your assistant, interested in photography do you know?"

"I don't know; but I don't think so!" exclaimed the jeweller, in a surprised tone. "Why?"

"Oh, I just asked!" laughed Blake. "Have you the addresses of all your assistants?"

"Yes; they are in the ledger."

"I would like them, from Ford, down to the night watchman. You don't know the address of either the man, Morris, or the woman, do you?"

"No. Morris just had his name on his card, and Miss Cole only gave me her name when I wrote the receipt."

"I see. You said she was driving a large red motor-car? Am I to understand there was no chauffeur?"

"Yes. She was all alone."

"I know Sir George Wallington, and, of course, he is out of the range of suspicion," went on Blake. "Just give me as close a description as possible of the two."

Bechstein did so, and the detective took the details down in his book.

A list of the addresses of all the employees was made up, and Blake thrust it into his pocket, with the pieces of the imitation necklace.

"I can't say when you will hear from me, Mr. Bechstein; but knowing how urgent the matter is, rest assured it will be as soon as I have anything definite to report."

"Thank you, Mr. Blake! It is of the greatest urgency. Don't let expenses stand in the way of pushing things."

Blake smiled as he held out his hand; but when he had gained the street, his brow knit in deep thought.

"From present indications," he muttered, "I can see no mistakes. The master brain behind this is unknown to me. Is it possible that what I have always expected has come— a scientist who practises crime as I practise its solution? If so—well, it will be a great chase."

AS Blake walked along absorbed in his thoughts, he was unaware of a veiled feminine figure noiselessly following him.

He hailed a taxi, and gave the driver his order, and, as the unsuspicious detective headed for Baker Street, the woman also hailed a cab, and followed closely.

Could he have known the tenor of her thoughts; he could that night have made a move which would have saved him from endless complications; but, unfortunately for him, and fortunately for the woman, he did not, and little did he dream he was the subject of these thoughts.

The woman wore a heavy veil; but, had she raised it, the reader would have recognised the girl of the yacht, for it was Yvonne.

Her eyes were thoughtful as she peered ahead through the window of the taxi.

"He looked like the pictures I have seen of Sexton Blake," she muttered to herself. "If Bechstein has put him on the case, I'll have to go warily. They say he is the cleverest-known detective; but it will take a cleverer man than you to trace me," she added, with a vindictive look at the front taxi. "I'll have to try to gain an entrance to his rooms on some pretext, in order to know more about him, for he must have assistants. It will be risky; but it's got to be done, and I'd better try to-night before he knows anything of me."

She sank back, only peering out again as they turned corners; but when the cab swung into Baker Street, she sat up with a jerk as the street sign caught her eye. She hastily took the speaking-tube from its hook, and signalled the driver.

"If the other cab stops, keep right on," she ordered. And a nod from the chauffeur told her he understood.

She was not a moment too soon, for barely had she returned the tube to its hook when the other taxi pulled into the kerb, and, as she went swiftly by, she saw the tall, slim figure of her quarry descending.

Once again Yvonne had recourse to the speaking-tube, and in obedience to her directions the chauffeur swung around a corner in a dark side street, coming to a stop a short distance up.

Yvonne dismissed the man, and stood motionless in the shadow until he was out of sight. But for herself the narrow street was vacant, and she moved slowly along, still keeping in the shadow.

A large house loomed up on her left, and the numerous placards, which decorated the front, told her it was to let. She tried the iron gate which led into the area, and muttered a word of relief as it yielded to her pressure. She glanced sharply up and down the street; but she was still the only wayfarer, and, again turning to the gate, she pushed it open. The gloom swallowed her up; but it was evident that she did not need light for her purpose, for she worked in silent haste, only a soft rustle betraying the presence of anyone amongst the shadows.

A few moments later there emerged from the area-way on elderly nun, who acted very peculiarly for one of that Order, for she glanced cautiously up and down the silent street before stepping forth.

With downcast eyes and slow step, the aged-looking Sister made her way towards Baker Street, and five minutes later rang the bell in front of Sexton Blake's apartments.

Something of moment disturbed her as she looked down, for she started visibly, and lifted her left hand quickly, but as the door was opened by the landlady she dropped it as quickly, and held it, with bent fingers, against the voluminous folds of her skirt.

Whatever she had intended doing had been prevented by the sudden opening of the door, and no other chance seemed to present itself before she was ushered a moment later into the consulting-room of the great detective.

Blake was sitting in his big chair before the fire as the nun was announced, while Tinker sat opposite, and Pedro lay between with one great eye open. All three rose as the Sister advanced into the room, and Blake bowed.

"I expect you are rather surprised to see one of my Order at nine o'clock at night," said the nun, with the slow enunciation of age, "but I know you are a busy man, Mr. Blake, and as I was in Baker Street I took the liberty of calling."

"I am accustomed to callers at all hours, Sister," smiled Blake, as he offered her a chair. "I trust there is nothing serious the matter?"

"Oh, no, indeed!" smiled back the nun, sinking into the chair. "Perhaps I shall not be so welcome when I tell you the object of my visit. I know you have a kind heart, Mr. Blake, and as we are making special efforts to send a large number of children to the seaside this summer, I am going to ask you to help us."

"With great pleasure," replied Blake, pulling out some notes. "Will ten pounds be of any use?"

"Yes, indeed, Mr. Blake," answered the nun, reaching for the notes. "You are very good. It will give a great deal of happiness to several poor children. And now I won't detain you any longer. I know you are a busy man, and must be tired," she added, as she rose and held out her hand.

"Not so busy as all that," laughed Blake, as he took her hand. "I trust you are successful in your endeavours. Poor children, they don't get much happiness, I'm afraid. Ah, a thousand pardons!" he exclaimed, as he knocked against a small tabouret, which fell over against the nun.

Tinker and Pedro had been silent listeners to the conversation, and the lad's eyes widened with surprise as the accident occurred, for Blake had had plenty of room to pass, and Tinker had never before known him to be clumsy.

The nun deprecated the matter as Blake straightened the tabouret, and, with a smile which included all three, she bowed and departed.

"I say, guv'nor," began Tinker, as the door closed behind her, "that was—"

"S-sh!" warned Blake, holding up his hand, and standing motionless until the nun's footsteps died away in the passage. "Get your cap and follow her, Tinker!" he ordered. "Be quick!"

Tinker sprang to his feet with a wondering stare, but he had been trained to obey orders without question. Blake spoke hurriedly as Tinker got ready.

"Don't lose sight of her for a moment. I'm not certain yet whether she is young or old. If she is young it is the most perfect disguise I have ever seen. But this I know, she is not a nun."

"Why? How—" began Tinker in astonishment.

"Hurry!" interrupted Blake. "She had forgotten to remove a ring from her left hand. She had evidently remembered it when too late, and I noticed that she kept her hand buried in the folds of her skirt. I wondered why, and thought it might be from habit, but in order to make sure I knocked over the tabouret. As I expected, she involuntarily lifted her hand to stop it, and I saw the ring on her finger. Nuns don't wear rings, and although she may be only a begging swindler, it is just possible— I'll explain that later," he broke off, as Tinker buttoned his coat. "You have plenty of money?" And as Tinker nodded, he went on: "Leave Pedro with me, for if she turned round she'd recognise him."

Tinker departed silently, and Blake moved to the desk with an expression of profound meditation.

"There's hardly a chance," he muttered, as he fingered a paper-knife. "No one would be so bold. I'm afraid I'm rating the perpetrator of the Bechstein robbery too high, but it certainly bears the marks of a great brain."

The thing was so unlikely that he could hardly consider it in his deductions, but it was typical of his great analytical mind that every suggestion of his instinct should be investigated. Many times had his brilliant reasoning advanced certain conjectures which, to the average mind, would seem meaningless and without connection, but scientific calculation told Blake that every abnormal happening might have a bearing on a subject, and the nun's visit was certainly to be classed as abnormal.

He resolved to wait up for Tinker's return, and, picking up a journal on photography, returned to the fire and began to read. Pedro sat up, and rested his head on Blake's knee, and the detective stroked the long ears as he read. Truly it was a scene of peace and comfort, but it did not last long. As Blake finished one article and turned to another, he suddenly stopped stroking the hound, his eyes grew tense with concentration as he hastily read the lines on the page before him.

It seemed a harmless article enough, for it dealt in a simple, forceful manner with advanced experiments on long distance photography, but it apparently held a deep interest for the detective.

"Extraordinary!" he muttered. "I didn't know there was anyone but myself working on that particular line of investigation. It shows a deep knowledge of the matter. It can't be Professor Greeley, for he is working on other lines. I'll write to the editor and ask who contributed the article."

Suiting the action to the word, he rose and moved over to the desk.

He wrote rapidly, and a moment later, with Pedro at his heels, he picked up his hat and went out to post the letter at a near-by pillar-box.

Blake sat for some time after his return, smoking his pipe, in deep thought. At intervals he rose and paced the room, followed by Pedro's watchful eyes. It was evident that a new thought was receiving consideration, and time passed unnoticed as he turned it over in its every phase.

Pedro's rising and stretching of his great legs recalled the detective, and he saw, with surprise, that the clock pointed to one o'clock.

"Tinker ought to have been here long before this," he muttered, as an anxious frown appeared. "I trust nothing has happened to him. But he's probably had a long chase. I'll wait up another hour—" But he broke off as he heard a ring, and knowing the landlady would be in bed he opened the door of his consulting-room, and moved down the passage to answer it.

He opened the door, and gazed with surprise as no one was visible, and, glancing down, he saw a folded piece of paper at his feet.

He bent down and picked it up. His eyes contracted, and his jaw set grimly, as he opened it, and saw the same ten-pound note which he had given the nun. It was unaccompanied by any writing whatsoever, and had been evidently thrust under the door by the person who had rung the bell.

"Every move shows a master mind," he muttered, as he scrutinised the note. "The extraordinary care taken to return this note proves it. A less clever mind would keep it, but this shows—"

The sudden jar of a starting motor sounded from some distance down the street, and Blake's teeth came together with a snap as two quick, decisive blasts on the horn told him he had been watched.

He dashed out to the kerb, and peered intently after the vanishing motor. As it passed under the light of a street lamp he saw that a solitary figure was driving, and from where he stood the colour of the car seemed to be—red!

TO return to Tinker. When he started out to follow the nun, he stood in the shadow as he reached the street, and was just in time to see a black-robed figure turn a corner.

With silent swiftness he sped after, and treaded warily as he reached the corner. No one was in sight as he cautiously peered around it, and thinking the nun had entered one of the houses, he was about to move along and endeavour to discover which one, when a dark figure emerged from an archway a short distance on, and turned in his direction.

Tinker hastily withdrew around the corner, and sank into the friendly gloom of a nearby doorway.

Hardly had he done so when the dark figure appeared, and a puzzled frown wrinkled the lad's face as he saw it was a stylishly-dressed woman, heavily veiled, and, from her walk, apparently young.

She passed without seeing him, and as she walked at a pace, Tinker had to think quickly.

"She's not much like the nun," he thought, "but I'll bet it's the same. She never had time to get any further up the street than where this one came from, but how she has changed so quickly—if it is the same—I don't understand. However, I don't dare risk losing sight of her to investigate, so I'll chance it and follow."

He kept to the dark part of the footpath where the buildings threw long shadows, and followed at a safe distance.

His quarry seemed to have a definite idea in mind, for she walked quickly, turning corners in rapid succession, and Tinker had his work cut out to keep up with her and not be discovered.

The chase led for several blocks, and Tinker looked in dismay as a solitary taxi appeared and his quarry hailed it.

He cast his eyes rapidly about for signs of another, and raised his arms quickly as one appeared around the corner. The other had already started, and was quickly gathering speed as he ran to meet the one he had hailed.

"Follow that taxi!" he gasped, as he threw open the door. "A half-sovereign over your fare if you keep it in sight!" The chauffeur needed no further inducement, and almost before the door slammed behind his fare he had thrown in the clutch and was speeding after the other.

Tinker leaned forward, and closely followed the progress of the chase, which led rapidly until the other taxi turned into Piccadilly. Up Piccadilly it went, and past Hyde Bark Corner to Knightsbridge.

Swinging around into Sloane Street, it slowed down, and Tinker hastily signalled his driver to keep on as the other drew into the kerb.

He looked back, and heaved a sigh of satisfaction as he saw the veiled woman get out and proceed in the same direction as he was taking.

His driver was still going at a good pace, and when several blocks had slipped by, Tinker signalled him to stop.

Slipping out as the taxi reached the kerb, he paid the man, and dismissed him. Far up the street he could see the dark figure of the woman still coming in his direction.

A hedge-lined street led off near at hand, and Tinker sought its shelter as the quick footsteps drew near.

As they came opposite and passed on, Tinker emerged from his hiding-place and once more took up the chase.

Through Chelsea they went until the leading figure turned down a narrow, dark street.

Rapidly the lad followed, and, turning the comer, he just had time to see a large motor-car standing a short distance up the street, and to notice that the woman had suddenly vanished, when he heard a soft rustle behind him, and he turned to find himself gazing into the shining barrel of a revolver which was held by the steady hand of the veiled woman.

"I wouldn't advise you to move," came a clear voice. "If you do, I will shoot without hesitation. I might inform you that this revolver is fitted with a new silencer, and the sound doesn't carry more than a few feet. Walk on, please, as far as that motor."

The crestfallen Tinker had nothing to do but obey; for the revolver was held in a very business-like grip, and the voice had spoken with decision.

"I'll watch my chance," he muttered, as he walked on with his captor uncomfortably close behind. "Maybe I'll be able to turn the tables. Heavens, what will the guv'nor say when I tell him I was fooled by a woman?"

He broke off to glance about for a chance of escape; but his heart sank as the tall figure of a man rose from the tonneau, where he had evidently been lounging on the seat cushions, for his head had not been visible from the rear.

"Hallo!" he exclaimed, as Tinker and his captor approached. "You're late. Who is this with you?"

"He is a persistent young man who has been following me. I tried to shake him off, but found he was too quick, so I brought him along, since he seemed so anxious for my company." And she gave a low laugh, which even Tinker, angry and disgusted with himself as he was, couldn't help but admire,

"What on earth are you going to do with him?" drawled the man, as he descended from the car. "He'll be an awful nuisance!"

"Oh, I'll take care of him all right!" she replied. "Just get those straps from under the seat, uncle, please, and tie him securely. Then put this in his mouth to keep him quiet." And she pulled a silk sash from under her jacket as she spoke.

The man followed her instructions, and a few minutes later the discomfited lad lay bound and gagged in the bottom of the tonneau.

He had kept his ears open as they talked, but noticed that they made use of no names.

"Well, anyway," he grumbled, as he nearly choked from the gag, "I know their relationship anyway. She called him uncle."

They had started to converse again, and Tinker strained his ears to listen, but the voices were too low for him to hear. As they ceased speaking, and the sound of departing footsteps reached him, he judged they were those of the man; and he was right.

He was ruminating on this point, and wondering what would happen next when he felt a quiver, and the car moved off. He tried to gain some idea of the direction by the turnings, but found it impossible, and, finally, gave it up.

He judged it to be fully half an hour later when the car came to a sudden stop, and he heard the driver descend and walk away. He knew positively then that is was the man who had left previously, for the present steps were the short, rapid ones of a woman.

As they grew fainter he struggled with his bonds, straining with all his strength; but they had been too cunningly tied, and again he sank back in despair. He had no idea where he was, and, as no sound of passing vehicles came to him, he judged he was either in a quiet side street, or in a suburb.

Little did he know that Blake was at that moment opening the street door not very far away, and that the panting figure which scrambled into the car at the same moment had just come from that door.

Two short blasts of the horn sounded as once more the car moved ahead, and Tinker wondered why the woman in the front seat laughed as she changed gears.

On they sped, and from the way in which they took corners, Tinker judged his captor was expert at driving. Two hours must have passed before she again brought the car to a stop, and Tinker wondered if they had reached their destination when the door of the tonneau opened, and his captor entered, and rapidly bound another silk sash around the captive's eyes, and, slamming the door again, started. They stopped in a few moments, and Tinker heard the sound of whispering as the tonneau door opened, and he was dragged to his feet. His legs were released, and he was led along blindfold. He was conscious of walking up some steps, and judged he was in a house or building of some description. His guide came to a halt, and the lad felt a current of air blow against his face as they started again.

"Look out, you're going down some steps!" growled his guide. And Tinker knew that the woman had turned him over to a man.

He felt his way cautiously as he descended, counting the steps as he went, and found, on reaching the bottom, that there were twenty-eight. Another journey followed, until once more his guide halted. He released the bandage from Tinker's eyes, and the lad blinked as a brilliant glare hit them. As the blurred picture cleared he looked about, and rapidly took in his surroundings.

He seemed to be in a small room, about twenty feet square. No windows of any description were visible, and his heart sank as he saw that the floor and walls, and even the ceiling were of stone. He looked towards the door; but no ray of hope lay in that direction, for it was of massive steel. The room was comfortably enough furnished—containing a small brass bed, covered with snowy linen.

A few rugs lay on the stone floor, and a well-filled bookcase lined one wall. In a corner stood an attractive desk, lit by the rays from an overhanging electric light. From the centre of the ceiling hung more lights, and in another corner was a marble wash-basin, with shining, nickelled faucets. Truly it was an impregnable prison—if prison it was.

As he finished his rapid survey of the room he looked at his guide, who was untying his bonds.

He had expected to see a ruffianly-looking fellow, and he opened his eyes wide as the man straightened up. He was dressed in a neat, blue uniform, with brass buttons, and had a distinctly nautical air about him.

He laughed as he saw the lad's look of surprise, and when he spoke it was with a suave intonation.

"Well, my lad," he smiled; "these are to be your quarters for some time. And, although there are no windows to admire the view, still you will find many entertaining books in the case—one in particular you ought to enjoy. It is a book of some of Sexton Blake's adventures. You won't be asked for your parole—"

"I wouldn't give it if I was," interrupted Tinker.

"As I was saying," went on the man imperturbably, "you won't be asked for your parole, because any efforts to escape are useless. Food will be served regularly to you, and you will remain here until further instructions are given regarding you. I might add"—and the man's eyes narrowed a trifle— "that if you do attempt to escape, I have instructions to deal summarily with you."

He moved to the door as he spoke, and Tinkers heart sank as the great steel barrier crashed to, and the bolts were shot.

WHEN Blake saw the fast-disappearing motor, he immediately connected it with the presence of the ten-pound note under his door.

He stood with knit brow watching it as it turned a corner.

Pursuit was out of the question. There was no taxi in sight. And besides, one of those low-geared cars would stand little chance of overtaking the big roadster.

The detective returned slowly to his room, and stood thinking deeply.

"Is it possible?" he muttered. "Red motor at Bechstein's—red motor to-night. The call of the nun, and the return of this note. Then that article in the journal. If there is the connection, I think my unknown antagonist must feel they have made a pretty safe retreat to dare to snap their fingers at me as the return of this note indicates. I can do nothing to-night. I'll leave the light for Tinker, in case he returns, and in the morning—well, my unknown friend, you have made the first move in the game." And his jaw set aggressively. "We'll see who calls checkmate. And by the way," he muttered, as he turned to seek his room, "if my deductions are correct, it proves that my unknown friend knew I was at Bechstein's, and had taken the case."

Blake was up betimes the next morning, and before sitting down to breakfast 'phoned for the big, grey car to be sent round.

He hastily perused his letters, and ran through the papers. He was depressed and worried over Tinker's non-appearance, and, as he donned his coat, Pedro looked at him with questioning eyes, and moved to the door ready to accompany him.

"It's all right, old chap!" said Blake. "We'll give him until to-night to return. He may have had a long chase; but if he isn't back, then we'll start to look for him."

Pedro wagged his tail in trustful understanding, and they descended to the waiting car.

Half an hour later Blake entered the office of the "Amalgamated Photographer," the well known journal on advanced photography

He was ushered into the office of the editor, who greeted him warmly.

"Well, well, this is an early call, Mr. Blake. Be seated. Have you brought us an article? It's some weeks since we received anything

50

from you, and, strange to say, I was about to write you and ask you to let us have something, if you were not too busy."

"I'm afraid I must disappoint you," laughed Blake. "I have really been too busy to write lately. But I see you have another contributor supplying you with articles on the same subject. I read one last night, and it interested me, as it showed the writer was following the same line of investigation which I am following. And that is really what brought me in this morning. Have you any objection to telling me the author's name?"

The editor's eyes had held a twinkle in them ever since Blake had entered; but as the detective made his request, he burst out laughing.

"You are fond of a joke, Mr. Blake. One would never think it, either. But I'll give in. Name your price, and I'll have the cashier' write you a cheque for them."

"Fond of a joke—name my price! I don't understand!" Blake said, with a puzzled look: "I assure you, Mr. Gordon, I am not joking in any way."

"Do you mean to say," asked the editor, sobering suddenly, "that you haven't been sending in those articles on long-distance, and embossed colour photography anonymously?"

"I assure you on my solemn word that I have sent in no anonymous articles." replied Blake.

"Well, I'm blest!" answered the other. "We've had four of them—bang up good articles, too! I thought all the time you were sending them in, and having a joke with us by not signing them. When you came in this morning I kept it up, pretended not to know they had come from you; but what you tell me is very surprising. Someone has been sending them in, and evidently they don't desire payment, for no name has come with them."

"As I have already said," remarked Blake, knitting his brows in deep thought. "I know nothing of them, and I have a particular reason for desiring to know who wrote them. Were the manuscripts typed?"

"Yes; all of them."

"I wonder if anyone in the office remembers what postmark was on the envelopes?" queried the detective.

"I hardly think so," replied the editor. "But I will see, if it is really important to you."

"I will be greatly obliged if you will—it is important."

"All right! I'll have Judd, the cashier in. He put the articles down to your credit, and may possibly have noticed the postmark; he's an observing old dog."

Gordon rang for the cashier.

He was tall, thin elderly man of nondescript appearance, except for a deep-set pair of keen grey eyes.

"Good-morning, Mr. Blake" he began, his eyes lighting up with pleasure. "I suppose you have dropped in to have the laugh on us, but we were too smart for you; we've credited them all up to you." And he shook his grey head as he chuckled.

"I'm afraid you are doomed to disappointment, Judd," laughed Blake. "Sorry to spoil the old man's pleasure, but I honestly didn't write those articles. I've just been telling Mr. Gordon."

"What?" gasped the cashier. "You didn't write them? Why—"

"No; we've made a mistake, Judd!" broke in the editor. "But Mr. Blake is very anxious to discover the author of them. You don't by any chance to remember the postmark?"

"Come to think of it, now I do remember. When the first one came in without any name, I naturally looked at the postmark. It was posted from Barnesley, in Surrey. I didn't notice the others, for you said they must have come from Mr. Blake, and that he was probably having a joke with us. I just credited them up to him."

"Good! Good!" exclaimed Blake. "Judd, you ought to have been a detective. It isn't much to go on, but it may help. I'm a thousand times obliged for the information."

"Not at all, not at all, Mr. Blake!" smiled the pleased cashier. "I'm glad if it is of any use."

"If any more come, I'll note the postmark, and let you know," said Gordon, as Judd withdrew. "Not professional jealousy I hope," he laughed; "but honestly, they were fine articles."

"No, something entirely different," replied Blake, rising.

"But you're right, I would say—yes, I would certainly say they emanated from a very brilliant, mind."

"They certainly did; and I could do with a few more of them. By the way I hope you will send us something soon."

"I will, shortly. And now I'll be getting along. Don't forget to note the postmark if anything else comes from your mysterious contributor, and do me the favour to say nothing about it, will you?"

"Right, I suppose, as usual, you have some unfathomable reason; but I'll say nothing."

Blake hastened to the street and climbed into the waiting car, where Pedro had remained on guard.

The detective threw in the clutch and threaded his way through the traffic of Fleet Street and into the Strand.

He stopped at a telegraph-office on the way and sent several messages.

He then turned the car towards Baker Street, little dreaming of the surprise that awaited him there.

54

WHEN the steel door clanged to, making Tinker a prisoner, he went over to it, but no sound penetrated through its thickness.

He sat down and considered things from every point of view, but his brain was too tired to solve the riddle.

He hadn't the faintest idea where he was, or what was the identity of the mysterious veiled woman. All he knew was that she was undoubtedly the same individual as the nun, and that he had followed the right person. Beyond that, and the fact that he was probably some distance out of London, he was all at sea.

Who his captors were—what they proposed to do with him, or in what way they were connected with Blake's investigations, he could not guess. He knew the detective was working on several cases, but Tinker did not know the details of the Bechstein robbery, as the nun had called so soon after Blake's return from Bond Street.

It was very late, and he was very tired; so, giving up the riddle for the time being, he undressed and slipped between the snowy sheets.

On the other side of the steel door was a scene which would have enlightened Tinker could he have witnessed it.

Yvonne sat in a large, stone-walled room, before a large mahogany desk. In another chair sat the man who had conducted Tinker to his prison. He was a clean-cut man, and it was obvious from his attitude that he was paying close attention to Yvonne's words.

The room was furnished as a mixture of laboratory and study. On one side were hundreds of technical and scientific books in glass cases, while on the other ranged the laboratory equipment. Wires of all sizes stretched across the ceiling, and instruments of brass and steel abounded everywhere. A large pillar rose from one corner, and on it was what looked like a very delicate instrument, for several very fine wires ran from it and disappeared through tiny holes in the stone walls. Yvonne consulted this instrument frequently, and she had just returned from one of her visits of inspection when we look in upon her.

"I don't think he'll come to-night." she remarked, as she resumed her seat before the desk. "If he had been able to get a car in time to follow, he would have been here by now."

"I don't imagine he will come at all," replied the man. "But you are marvellous. Miss Cartier!" he went on, with a deeply admiring glance. "I never thought I'd turn criminal; but honestly, it's a pleasant surprise to find it so interesting. I always had an idea that criminals wore a hang-dog look and were coarse ruffians, but without doubt the world moves."

"I have certainly been fortunate in finding a reliable ally like you to take charge of the yacht and assist me, Captain Vaughan," answered Yvonne, with her silvery laugh. "But I promised to explain to you to-night the workings of the 'ear instrument.' " And, rising again, she led the way to the instrument in the corner which she had been consulting with such regularity.

"I will give you the necessary technical notes which will explain it thoroughly," she went on. "But roughly, the idea is this."

She then proceeded to describe in detail the delicate instrument which was the product of her brilliant mind, and certainly no one would have thought the beautiful, bronze-haired girl, who stood talking with such a profound knowledge of science, was probably the cleverest, and for that reason the most to be feared, criminal living. She had started with a strong motive, but the fascination of the game had seized her, and she pursued it now for the love of it. She had developed into more than an adventuress. Her wonderful brain had studied incessantly with extraordinary patience until she ranked with the greatest scientists of the day. This knowledge she brought to bear on her operations, and everything was planned with mathematical precision and detail before she embarked on it.

"So, you see," she said, as she finished her demonstration, "that is really on the same lines as Mapim's invention for ships. These wires carry the waves outside for a radius of sixty feet in all directions. Any moving object in that radius comes into contact with the waves, and the movement is reflected back on this register. That is the reason I had all the trees cleared away in order that the moving of the branches would not reflect on the register. Consequently you can see how I could easily discover if anyone approached the house."

"Marvellous!" murmured her companion. "It makes a remarkable watchdog for you!"

"It does, indeed," smiled Yvonne, as she returned to her seat, "Yes, I feel quite secure in my retreat. The cleverest man in the world could roam over the house above, and he would never discover my underground apartments. But this man Sexton Blake must be stopped!" she went on, her eyes hardening. "He is unlike other detectives, and has a wonderful mind. I think I have planned my retreat too well for him to discover me; but at the same time, one never knows when he may stumble on something, and for that reason he will have to be watched."

"What, will you do?" asked Taylor.

"I'm going to take the bull by the horns and invade his rooms. He will have made notes, and I may be able to get a look at them."

"But that will be impossible, won't it?" protested the captain.

"No, I'll manage it all right. If I am discovered—well, society will lose one of its most shining members, for I wouldn't permit Sexton Blake, or anyone else, to interfere with my plans. And now, captain, I want you to slip in and see if my captive is asleep. If he is, bring all his clothes out to me, for I will need them."

The mystified captain did as he was bid, and returned a few moments later with Tinker's clothes in his arms.

"He was sound asleep!" he chuckled, as he dropped them.

"He'll be surprised in the morning when he finds his clothes gone!"

"You'd better take in some of uncle's, and leave them for him." remarked Yvonne, "and then go to the yacht. Tell uncle to come up here, and you'd better keep steam up. If things come to a crisis between this man Blake and I; I might, need to get away quickly."

"Very well," he replied. "I trust you won't come into conflict with him. He's a dangerous man."

"I'll take care of myself all right." she laughed; but her companion wore a worried look as he departed.

Immediately he had gone, Yvonne closed the door and moved to the mirror. She uncoiled her beautiful bronze hair, and. reaching for a jar, applied some greasy substance to it.

Its thick, wavy folds clung together as though wet, and when she tucked it under a close-fitting, flesh-coloured skull-cap, it lay down flat.

"Let me see!" she murmured, as she walked over to a large cabinet. "He has brown hair, hasn't he?"

Opening the cabinet, a large stock of wigs of all shades were displayed, and, choosing one of a brown colour, she placed it on her head. She next moved to the door, and opening it, hastened down the passage to the room where Tinker slept. Softly slipping the bolts and switching on the light, she entered, and moved over to the sleeping lad. She earnestly studied his face, feature by feature, and, apparently satisfied with her scrutiny, she left as noiselessly as she had come.

On her return to the laboratory, she went again to the mirror. A few touches here and there, and a rearrangement of the wig changed her fresh, girlish face into the more boyish duplicate of Tinker's. Slipping off her dress she struggled into Tinker's garments, and five minutes later glanced at her reflection with satisfaction. And well she might, for she stood a perfect reproduction of the sleeping lad.

"It wouldn't deceive Blake," she muttered "but it will get me past the landlady all right. I hope the dog isn't there, it might be awkward."

She placed Tinker's cap on her head, and switching out the light, left the room. She went through the stone passage, turning off the lights in several luxuriously-furnished rooms as she passed, stopping for a moment in one to pick up a revolver, which she slipped into her pocket. Up a flight of stone steps she went, and on reaching the top, turned out the last light.

She pressed a button, and a huge, stone door swung back noiselessly. Passing through as the door swung to behind her with a soft click, she emerged into a wide, old-fashioned fireplace such as are common in ancient houses. It opened into a small, meagerly-furnished cottage sitting-room, and through an open door could be seen a cottage parlour, its quaint furniture looking ghostly in the just breaking dawn.

It was a harmless-looking cottage, and might have belonged to any small farmer. Little would one think such a luxurious retreat lay beneath it.

The old stable, to which Yvonne directed her steps, was equally innocent-looking. The floor was half-covered with empty bins, but what was not known to casual observers was that on the bottom of each bin was a small, innocent-looking metal strip which lay over the big spikes in the rough-looking planking.

A curious mind would find it quite possible to move the bins freely about, but he would not know that through those spikes at times caught a high current of magnetism, which held the bins firmly to the floor on certain occasions. And this was one of the occasions, for as Yvonne entered the door she reached her hand up to a small nail in the wall, and gently pressed.

One side of the floor dropped, while the other rose, and the bin-covered farm floor turned completely over on a pivot, bringing into view a smooth steel floor on which was a large red motor held to by clamps. The whole movement could not have been heard ten feet away. It was ingenious, to say the least, and certainly Yvonne had gone to great pains to secure a safe retreat.

She released the clamps which held the motor in place when the floor had been upside-down, and, pressing the starting button, backed out of the stable. She sprang out, and once more pressed the small nail on the wall, and again the rough, bin-covered floor appeared, the current which had held them being cut off as the floor swung back into place.

Springing into the driving-seat, she threw in the clutch, and, with a last parting glance at the innocent-looking farm cottage, headed for London.

YVONNE reached Baker Street about eight o'clock, and swung the car up a side street, where she pulled up. Springing out, she strolled casually to the corner, and a gleam of satisfaction came into her eyes as she saw a large grey car a short distance up the street.

She hastened back to her own car, and, after looking carefully around the quiet side street, she reached forward and turned a small button. A quick "slushing" sound followed, and the red coat which had thrown back the morning sun flashed up and out of sight like the cover of a roll-top desk, leaving a dark-blue coloured body instead.

"I might need to change twice," she muttered, as she reached once more for the button. Again the slushing noise followed as the blue coat disappeared under the overhanging rolled edges, and a grey appeared. With the driver so much like Tinker, it did not look unlike Blake's machine, and Yvonne smiled to herself as she noticed the similarity.

Once more she strolled to the corner, and loafed casually for some time.

As Blake appeared and entered his car, she hurried back to her own, and bent over out of sight as Blake swept past the corner.

She straightened after he had flashed by, and climbed into the seat.

Patiently she sat, and the occasional passer-by never looked twice at the whistling boy lounging in the seat.

Half an hour passed before Yvonne made a move. She slipped from the car and walked to Baker Street, quickening her footsteps as she turned the corner. Pulling from her pocket a small bunch of keys which she had taken with Tinker's clothes, she rapidly tried them one after the other, and heaved a sigh of relief as the lock yielded.

She hastened down the passage, and opened the door of the consulting-room where she had been the previous evening. She wasted no time, and moved at once over to the desk, but stopped as her eye fell on the photographic journal which lay uppermost on the table where Blake had thrown it the previous night.

Quickly snatching it up, she turned the leaves, and her eyes narrowed as she saw the pencilled criticisms which Blake had made in the margin.

"So he's up in that, is he?" she muttered. "You're cleverer than I thought, Mr. Blake, but I guess you're not clever enough to find the author of that article or to connect it with Mr. Bechstein."

She carefully replaced the magazine as she had found it, and continued towards the desk. Rapidly she ran her eye over the contents, and she was reaching for a small notebook when the sound of a motor stopping outside came to her ears.

Yvonne swung round, and crept softly to the window. As she peered through the curtain she saw a big grey car from which Sexton Blake and Pedro were just descending. Her heart stood still for a moment, and she cast about rapidly for a place of escape. Rushing to the door, she opened it and looked up and down the passage. No one was in sight, and she closed the door behind her and sped down it as her eye caught sight of a small door at the lower end. It looked like a cupboard, and she was right, for as she pulled it open and sprang in she stumbled over a pile of linen.

Yvonne just had time to close the door when the click of a key sounded at the street entrance, and she heard Blake's steps come down the passage and enter the consulting-room,

Blake made straight for the photographic journal as he entered, intending to read the article over again, but paused to glance curiously at Pedro, who was running about the room, sniffing excitedly.

"What is it, old chap?" asked the detective, puzzled by the dog's unusual actions.

Pedro only pounded his tail, and kept on sniffing. Blake turned sharply as the hound suddenly lifted his head and dashed at the closed door.

"Better give him his head and see what bothers him," muttered Blake, moving across and opening the door. As Pedro dashed out, the detective followed, and as he did so he looked up the passage as he heard the street door click.

"Strange!" he muttered, as Pedro dashed down the passage to the cupboard and back to the front, entrance.

"Somebody must have gone out, and, from Pedro's actions, whoever it was must have been in the consulting-room. It wasn't the landlady, for Pedro never pays any attention to her. I wonder—" He broke off, and, dashing to the door, threw it open, and hastened out to the footpath. The figure of a lad running caught his eye, and he gasped in amazement as he took it at first sight for Tinker, but as it turned the corner he called back Pedro, who had started in pursuit, and, jumping into the car, which stood at the kerb, started after.

"Good heavens!" he muttered, as he threw in the clutch and turned recklessly. "I could almost have sworn it was Tinker except for the run. The lad never ran like that, but one thing is certain. There is some deep game on, and Tinker has fallen a victim to it, for I'll swear those were his clothes. I'm up against a shrewd antagonist, for whoever it is has dared to enter my flat and search it."

He turned the corner as his musings reached this point, and increased the speed as he saw the imitation Tinker leap into another grey car and dash off at breakneck speed.

Blake was more convinced than ever of the clever brain against him, and he settled down over the wheel for the chase with a savage gleam in his eye. It boded no good for the fugitive ahead if he were caught, for Blake was irritated by the boldness of his unknown enemies; and, to make matters worse, he was so far completely in the dark as to their identity.

He had, of course, his ideas on the subject, and was working on those lines, but he had started without a clue of any sort in the real sense of the word, and the slender threads on which he was working would have seemed ridiculous to anyone else. He knew, however, that he was up against a big hidden force, and no doubt remained in his mind that it was connected with the Bechstein robbery. He knew every move he made was probably watched, and his eyes grew anxious as he thought of Tinker in the hands of the enemy.

"I'd give something to know who is behind it all!" he muttered, as he followed the other car, which was going in violation of all speed laws. "But I won't rest until I do, and when I know—well—" And the detective's jaw finished the thought.

On dashed the two powerful grey cars, and Blake risked a further increase of speed as he saw the quarry head for the Strand.

"If I don't keep close I'll lose it in the traffic," he thought.

The leading car eased up as it entered the narrow, crowded Strand, and Blake did likewise. He was gaining, however, and trusted to his power with the traffic police to get him through if a blockade occurred.

He sent the car forward, and swung around as the other turned a corner. As he did so his brow knit in puzzlement, for ahead of him, it is true, was a big motor, but it was not grey like the one he had been following, but blue, and instead of a boy at the wheel the driver appeared to be a man, for he was wearing a black bowler hat.

The amazed detective pulled up as he came to the entrance of a courtyard, and, jumping out quickly, surveyed the inner enclosure. His examination was fruitless, however, and he dashed back.

"It's a poser," he muttered, "but it must be the same. Another proof of their cleverness. I'll have a job to overtake it." he thought. He sent the car forward again, and followed on. There was only one turning, and it led to the left and thence round to the Strand again. Blake followed, and as he reached the street he saw a blue car just speeding towards the Law Courts. It had a solitary driver, and although he now wore a soft hat, Blake swung after.

As the detective threaded his way through the thundering 'buses, his already exasperated temper would have blazed had he seen a big red motor enter the Strand shortly after from the same street from which Blake had come, for the wily Yvonne had seen the blue car, and, risking Blake's following it, she had circled right around the way she had come, and, pressing the button, threw down the red coat before she emerged.

She chuckled as she saw Blake driving after the other, and, turning, headed swiftly in the opposite direction.

Blake over took his quarry as he reached the Law Courts. As he came up behind he took note of the number. He had been unable to catch the number of Yvonne's car, but as he memorised what he thought was it a doubt filled his mind, for the back of the driver's head looked vaguely familiar.

He pressed the horn sharply, and, as the other involuntarily turned, Blake gasped in disgusted amazement as he recognised the well-known profile of Inspector Kelly of Scotland Yard. Rapidly he pulled alongside, and signed to the inspector to stop.

"Hallo, Blake!" called the inspector, as he pulled up. "Did you wish to speak to me?"

"Yes, for a moment," replied Blake. "Which way have you just come?"

"Straight up Whitehall, and through the Strand. Why?" asked the inspector, in surprise.

"Did you leave the Strand at all?" continued Blake.

"No. As I told you, I came straight along. Anything wrong?"

"No. I took you for someone else," answered Blake. "Sorry to have troubled you."

"He seems savage," grinned the inspector, as Blake turned and drove off. "Wonder what bothers him? Maybe someone has given him the slip. If that's the case, and he followed me in mistake, no wonder he's wild. Ha, ha! That's a good one on him if it's so! I'll pass it on to the chief." And the inspector, still chuckling, continued on his way.

Blake returned direct to Baker Street. His face was set sternly as he entered the consulting-room. Pedro took up his place by the fire, and watched his master with anxious gaze as the latter paced rapidly up and down. The detective lunched lightly, and afterwards carefully re-read the article in the photographic journal.

Bechstein rang up on the 'phone soon after, and the detective told him shortly to drop around in two days' time as he was moving in the matter that night.

During the afternoon several telegrams arrived, in answer to the ones he had sent early in the morning, and all were of the same tenor.

"None of the employees interested in photography. That settles it." he muttered, as he read the last.

He filled his pipe, and not until the shadows lengthened did he move.

Rising, he donned a heavy coat and cap, and, slinging a revolver in his pocket, told the disappointed Pedro to watch things, and left the house. His face was still grim as he climbed into the car, and headed the powerful monster for Surrey.

THE EIGHTH CHAPTER.   On the Trail.

IT was a chilly evening; but Blake was too absorbed in his thoughts to pay any attention to the weather. Mechanically he drove the delicately-tuned car which had been through so many adventures with him, and where the road was clear he put on full speed.

The detective's deductions were, it is true, based on a very slender thread, but beyond this slender thread absolutely no trace of a clue existed. Three people had inspected a certain necklace in a certain jewellery establishment in Bond Street. None of them had had it in their hands for more than a few seconds. It had only been in the establishment for about three weeks, and yet, strange to say, when it was examined at the end of that time it was discovered to be a forgery. And what a forgery—every tiny detail had been reproduced perfectly, even down to the bent filigree clasp.

On first thoughts it would seem unlikely that the false necklace could have been reproduced while the genuine one lay at Bechstein's. Consequently, the step would lead back to the point from which it originated. Blake had naturally followed that line of reasoning, but had discarded the hypothesis after a conversation with Craig, the head of the big firm which had supplied the necklace to Bechstein.

"No," Mr. Craig had said, "there would be no possibility of the article being duplicated here, Mr. Blake. I myself selected the pearls as they came in, and my brother drew the design for the settings and clasp. Both gems and designs were kept in the private safe, and until they were brought out to set, no one had access to them but my brother and myself. The setting was all done by a man who has been with the firm for over thirty years, and each night he brought everything to be put back in the safe, for even with us this was a good-sized order, and we gave it every care. The very day they were finished they were delivered to Bechstein, so any duplication must have taken place while they were at his place."

Blake ran over the conversation as the car pounded over the quiet country roads, and again he eliminated the possibility of the duplication at Craig's. It would require a long time to make the design for the settings and the filigree clasp, let alone the pearls, which require even longer. As far as Blake could see the whole thing could hardly be done in three weeks. He had carefully investigated the possibility of any of the assistants having sufficient access to the safe, but Ford was the only one, and the investigation of his affairs had yielded nothing bearing the slightest suspicious element.

From that point the circle narrowed to two elements—one of which was the possibility of Bechstein having duplicated the necklace himself—but that also had been cast out by the detective, for mathematically it was not possible. Bechstein's distress had been too genuine, and he would not willingly cut his own throat financially, and Blake's investigations of the jeweller's financial affairs had yielded the fact that Bechstein spoke the truth when he said, if the necklace was not recovered in a few days he would go the wall.

No; only one thread remained, and as has been said, it was so fine that even Blake's keen reasoning barely grasped it. But his system of analysing had cast out any others, and, true to his nature, he seized the only thread exposed. Whether it was strong enough to connect up and tie the loose ends of the circle remains to be seen. In any event, he would follow it until it led to something else, or broke in mid-air to use his own expression.

But he frankly acknowledged to himself that the whole matter presented less material to work on than any case he had ever had. He still persisted in his theory that no criminal, no matter how clever and scientific, was capable of organising and committing a crime, and making a retreat without a single mistake. He stubbornly held to that, although the present case seriously jarred his theory.

Tinker's disappearance worried him, and proved that a strong unknown force had started to work against him from the moment he took up the case. Certainly every detail bore the stamp of a master brain, which used methods complied to those of the ordinary criminal, as the automatic pistol is to the ancient blunderbuss.

But he would stick to the chase until he either succeeded or was beaten and the steady look of his eyes made it obvious that that would be only when life departed.

With this culmination of the working of his mind he entered the village of Barnesley.

Barnesley was a mill village, and, consequently, the individual dressed as a mill-hand, which quietly slipped out of the back door of the inn, and entered the bar an hour later created no curiosity, as he freely mingled with the other customers.

One of their many grievances was being aired by a talkative individual, and the disguised Blake, anxious to gain all knowledge he could without causing comment, listened as he carelessly sipped a glass of beer.

"I says as 'ow it ain't fair," the speaker was saying, in a slightly-thick voice "'Ere we hare workin' like blessed slaves for wot? I ses for wot?"

His companions seemed more interested in their beer than in his meandering, and no one volunteered "wot " they were working for. But the speaker was not discouraged by the lack of interest, and kept on, himself supplying the answer to his question.

"I'll tell yer for wot," he hiccoughed. "For a bloomin' 'ard bed, and bloomin' little food, and bloomin' little beer, and—"

"Sounds like a rose garden with all your bloomin's," put in a facetious listener; but the orator waved his remark aside with a contemptuous snort, and continued unabashed.

"Yuss, an' wot do them for who the likes of us works get? I arsk you, brethren?"

"Oh, shut up, and have a beer!" growled a burly good-natured-looking man on a form. "We gets paid for our work, and I know at the present time if higher wages had to be paid the mill would have to shut down."

"Again I arsk you!" persisted the inebriated one. "Wot do they get? Look at the man wot drove that big, grey car to-day. Does he work as hard as we do? I'll bet 'e don't know wot work is. Prob'bly the gilded son of some useless rich man."

Blake smiled into his glass at this description of himself, while the orator leered with satisfaction at his own words.

"An' look at all the other idle rich wot do nothin' but run round in motor-cars, and 'unt. There's that party wot dashes through the village in 'er big, red car as though we was all dogs, to go scampering out of her way. Only to-night she drew up the road to the station, and I had to move bloomin' quick to save myself. I tell yer again—"

But what he was going to tell them again ended in a gurgle as the big man on the form reached forth a mighty hand, and unceremoniously dragged the speaker down, where he lay in undignified discomfiture.

In the general laugh which followed none of them saw the gleam in the eyes of the strange mill-hand when the drunken orator spoke of the "red car an' 'er." Quietly he finished his beer, and unobtrusively slipped out while the laugh still kept on.

"I wonder—I wonder," he said softly, as he quickened his steps and hastened in the direction of the railway-station, "if this is a lengthening of the thread, or only a profitless chase?"

He swung up the road leading to the railway, and almost ran as he heard the whistle of the evening train. He was too far away to see if anyone descended, and stopped in the shadow as the train quickly started again. The purr of a motor had come to his ears, and he sank back still further as the brilliant headlights shone down the road. A moment later it swept past him at high speed, but not before Blake had seen that it contained three occupants—one of whom was at the driving-wheel, and it looked like a woman, and he also saw that the colour was red.

Hastily he gathered himself up as the motor sped on, and he started on a run in pursuit, not stopping until he had reached the top of a hill. Here he paused, and gazed intently through the night until he saw the lamps appear on the main road below. He watched them until they reached the cross-roads, and turned to the left, and not until then did he relax his tense attitude.

For a man who seemed as interested as he had been in the appearance of the motor, Blake descended the hill at a strangely-leisured pace.

He walked with apparent indifference down the main street of the village, pulling up as the solitary constable appeared.

"Good-evening!" remarked Blake, as that worthy passed. "A fine evening!"

"None 'o yer smartness," growled the constable. "You mill fellers are getting too cheeky to the law." And he drew himself up with puffing dignity as he delivered himself of the words.

Blake laughed, and, turning, strolled along beside the other. He spoke a few words to that individual as they walked along, and the policeman turned to reply sarcastically when he paused as he saw the look in the mill-hand's eyes.

"You're bluffin'—" he began.

"I don't blame you for doubting," interrupted Blake; "but come with me to the inn, and I will prove it."

"I'm sorry, sir," apologised the officer, as he recognised the ring of authority in Blake's voice. "You see, sir, these fellow's of the mill are always trying to put up a game on me, and I have to be careful. But I'm mighty proud to meet you, sir—that I am," he said, his eyes lighting with pride. "But no one would ever know you in that get up, sir. I've mixed with these mill men all my life, and I'd never have known the difference."

"All right, officer!" laughed Blake, good-naturedly. "Come along to the inn! I'd like some information from you!"

A few moments later Blake and the policeman entered the inn by the side door, and went quickly to the detective's rooms.

If the policeman had any lingering doubts as to Blake's identity they were dissipated on Blake's return in usual garb from his bedroom, where he had gone at once on entering.

He quickly put the now embarrassed constable at his ease, and, offering him a cigar, lit one himself.

"Now, officer," he began, "I'm down here on a little private investigation, and if you care to assist me, you won't be the loser by it. By the way, what is your name?"

"Hobbs is my name, sir; and I'd be proud to work with you without any reward for it," replied the constable. "Anything I can do, Mr. Blake, I'll be glad to do."

"Thank you," smiled Blake. "But remember, please, that for the present everything I say is strictly between ourselves."

"I understand, sir," replied the flattered constable.

"Did you see the big red motor-car which was in the village?" asked Blake.

"Oh, yes, sir!" answered Hobbs. "It often comes in."

"Do you know who owns it?"

"I can't say I do, sir. Sometimes a lady drives it, and sometimes a man—middle-aged he is. I'd know their names if they lived in my district, but I think they must live over Colby way. Hanson has that district, but he makes Creighton his headquarters."

"Why, then, would they come here instead of to Creighton?" asked Blake.

"I imagine, sir, because the London express stops here and doesn't at Creighton,"

"I see," mused Blake. "Do you know Colby well?"

"Oh, yes, every foot of it!" answered Hobbs. "I've often relieved over there."

"You'd know, then, all the residents, of course?''

"Yes, indeed. I got to know it pretty well during the Granger murder there six years ago. I was at the Granger Farm for some time during the investigation."

"You wouldn't know, of course, at what place those people live in the Colby district?"

"No, sir, I wouldn't. I've always imagined they must be on a visit. I don't know of any vacant places or any that have changed except the old Granger Farm, and, of course, these people wouldn't live at a place like that. Besides, no one will go near it since the murder."

"I see!" again muttered Blake. He subsided into silence, and puffed his cigar thoughtfully for some time.

"Well, Hobbs, as I said, keep quiet for the present. In the meantime I'll think over things to-night, and will communicate with you in the morning."

"Very good, sir," replied Hobbs, rising to leave; and as the door closed Blake threw himself into a chair, and smoked in deep absorption over a road map until long after midnight.

THE NINTH CHAPTER.   Blake is Captured.

BLAKE was astir early the next morning, and started in the big car for Colby village.

He had left a note for Hobbs telling him to keep quiet until his return.

His ideas might be without foundation, but he decided to test them, and, with that end in view, had made an early start.

He reached Colby village early in the afternoon, and an hour later left the inn dressed in tweeds and a cap. He struck across country, and as the afternoon waned and dusk closed down he came in sight of the deserted Granger farmhouse.

It looked desolate and cheerless, but that evidently did not detract from its interest for Blake, for he dropped into some thick bushes, and turned his gaze on the old place.

Over two hours passed, and still the detective did not move. Darkness had shut down some time ago, and the house was now invisible, but he still kept his gaze in its direction. Another half-hour passed, and the silent figure stirred as a sudden light flashed and disappeared. It came from the direction of the house, and Blake leaned tensely forward as it appeared the second time. The light moved along for a short distance, and again disappeared. Two minutes later two brilliant lights gleamed forth, and Blake smiled in grim satisfaction.

"The motor!" he breathed, as he stood up in the shelter of the trees, and watched the lights as they swung round and headed away from the house. When they had disappeared, he sank back, and watched patiently for another half-hour before he moved.

"I'll try it now," he muttered, as he rose. "They may come back at once, and, on the other hand, they may have gone to London. It's a funny place to hang out, and it's a risky proposition to investigate it alone, but it's got to be done. Who knows, poor Tinker may be in that house? It's a flimsy place, and if it belongs to whom I think it does it doesn't seem in order with their usual cleverness!"

Unfortunately for Blake, he did not know at that time just how clever his unknown antagonists really were, and although he knew he was running a great risk in investigating that lonely place by himself, he didn't dream of the complete system and luxurious retreat hidden away under that lonely farmhouse.

He crept cautiously, picking his steps, and noiselessly parting the branches as he went.

Dropping to the ground as he reached a large clearing, he could just distinguish the black bulk of the house and stable.

"It doesn't look very inviting," he thought, as he took a careful reconnoitering look around before proceeding.

"Seems deserted, too. Perhaps there's nobody at home. However, here goes!" And he began to creep stealthily forward over the open ground.

Little did Blake know that as he crawled through the short grass toward the creepy blackness of that desolate house, that almost underneath him, in a luxuriously-furnished stone-walled apartment, sat an alluring bronze-haired girl with narrowed eyes and scornful smile, intently watching a small machine set in one corner, on which a delicate needle was quivering, registering every movement the detective made.

The watching woman muttered a smothered exclamation, and rose to her feet as the needle swung round half-way.

"I wish uncle and Hendricks would hurry," she muttered, as she went over to the desk and picked up a revolver. "It may be only some prowling tramp, but, on the other hand, that man Blake may have stumbled on something. However, I'll have to chance it!"

Switching out the lights, she slipped off her shoes, and, gripping the revolver, stole noiselessly along the passage and up the stairs. She turned out the passage lights as well, although it was a needless precaution, for not the faintest ray could penetrate from that perfectly-built retreat.

Yvonne stood listening for some time, but as no sound came from the interior of the cottage on the other side of the stone door, she pressed the releasing button, and the perfectly balanced door swung silently open.

Creeping through, with infinite caution, Yvonne dropped flat, and lay, scarcely breathing, as the almost imperceptible click of the closing door sounded behind her. Holding before her the hand which held the revolver, she crept out of the fireplace and across the floor to the door of the room. Softly she turned the latch, and caught her breath with a jerk as it made a very slight noise which sounded like the report of a gun to her taut nerves.

Again she lay still, listening for sounds, but none came, and she continued her creeping progress. Over the short grass went the dark figure, ever keeping the revolver pushed in front, until the black shadow of the stable loomed up. On reaching one comer she dropped back and held her breath. Her teeth showed for a moment as a slight shuffling sound reached her ears. Slowly, and feeling cautiously every inch, she crept into the dark entrance. From inside came no sound; now and again she dropped to the ground.

Silence still reigned from inside the stable, and she dared not move, for she knew not in what direction the intruder might be creeping.

The intruder had a very good reason for keeping silent, for his instinct, almost as soon as his quick ears had realised the presence of another being somewhere in the surrounding darkness. He also had dropped down, and lay scarcely breathing, for he was as yet uncertain whether the sound emanated from somewhere inside the dark stable or came from the outside.

It was one of the strangest positions in which either had ever found themselves. Only a thin wall separated the cleverest detective of crime and the cleverest female perpetrator of crime that the world had over known. Both of those brilliant brains were working rapidly to devise some scheme to make the hidden foe make the first move, and in the meantime the deadly sinister silence reigned, heavy with the portent of the coming struggle.

As is usually the case, the woman's mind worked more rapidly. Its decisions are not always the soundest, but in this case it was a brilliant stroke.

To fully appreciate the situation, it must be remembered that, as usual, the bin-covered side of the floor had been swung back into place as the motor departed, and it was in this confused array that Blake lay. He was on foreign ground, and up until now had carried on his investigations by darkness, as he had considered it unsafe as yet to use a light. And in that moment he congratulated himself on his forethought, but, alas! it only saved him for the moment.

Outside lay Yvonne within a few feet of the open door. Only the thin wall of the stable separated them, and where they lay they were only a few inches from one another. Yvonne acted quickly once she had made her decision. Regardless of noise, she dashed to her feet and bounded madly for the open door. As the dark figure entered, Blake lifted his revolver, and suddenly, seeing the shape of the figure, hesitated to fire, for in the dense gloom he thought, and rightly, it looked like a woman. He could not fire, but he could take her prisoner forcibly, and, stuffing his revolver in his pocket, leaped forward.

But Yvonne's fingers had found the small nail in the familiar wall. Feverishly she pressed it, and sprang back, firing into the darkness as she did so.

As the bullet whistled past Blake's head, he felt the floor suddenly sink from under him. He reeled and stumbled, then gathered himself together on his hands and knees, gripping wildly in the dark for something to hold on to. Lower went the floor, a brilliant light flashed, giving him a lightning view of a tangle of gold bronze hair above a white, gleaming skin, and as the floor swung still lower and turned completely over he dropped into the void below, passing into unconsciousness to the sound of a silvery, mocking laugh.

TINKER had spent two miserable days in his prison.

True, he had been served very good food at intervals by a woman, who pushed it through a cunningly-devised, opening in the steel door, and the bookcase was filled with many interesting volumes.

He had been getting around in a suit of clothes about five sizes too big for him, and he could only judge the time by the regular arrival of the meals. Otherwise it was impossible to tell whether it was day or night, for no windows were let into his stone prison. How the place was ventilated Tinker had been unable to discover, but a pure current of air flowed through constantly from some invisible source.

He was disgusted at his capture by a woman, and worried on Blake's account, and at the end of the second day he paced the room in his big, loose garments, with his brow wrinkled savagely. He was certainly in a very unpleasant frame of mind, and, from his point of view, he had reason to be.

It is hard to guess what his feelings would have been had he known that at that moment Blake was creeping over the ground within a very short distance of him.

The lad had seen none of his captors since his arrival with the exception of the woman who handed in his meals, and all attempts to draw her into conversation had failed.

Consequently, although he knew not the reason, he was relieved to hear the bolts spring back in the door, and he swung round as it opened.

He gasped in astonishment as he saw the beautiful woman who entered, and his fascinated-gaze barely noticed the two men who followed, bearing an apparently lifeless body.

He tore his gaze from the woman, and every thought but one fled from his mind as he saw that the body was Blake's. He gave a strangled cry as it was laid on the bed, and, rushing over, knelt beside it. Feverishly he felt the cold wrists, and pressed his ear to the apparently still heart.

He gasped with relief as he heard it beat faintly, and, springing to his feet, swung on his captors. He recognised the elder of the two men as the man who had descended from the motor the night he was captured. The other man was dressed in nautical uniform, but he was not the same who had conducted Tinker to his prison.

The lad was burning with deep distress and indignation, and he almost choked as he blazed out at them, but he did not notice the curious look in the woman's eyes as he spoke.

"If any evil befalls the guv'nor from your fiendish schemes, I'll—I'll kill you all, if it takes me all my life to find you!" The lad's voice broke as he struggled manfully to control the sob of distress that would break out. But he gazed in surprise as the beautiful woman spoke.

"Don't worry, my lad," she said gently. "Your guv'nor, as you call him, will have his life spared this time. He took his life in his hands when he came to this place, and I had intended making it cost him that life. But this time—and remember it is only for this time;—I will spare it. I have memories," she added, more to herself, "See what you can do, uncle, to bring him round; and you, Hendricks, go, please, to the laboratory and bring me the blue jar in the left-hand corner of the top case."

She moved to the brass bed as she finished speaking, a look of brooding sadness in her eyes. Her thoughts were far away in a grief-laden, ranch house in sunny Australia; but as they swung round to the people who had caused her to adopt the kind of life she led, she almost regretted her momentary generosity.

Long and earnestly she gazed at the strong, still face beneath her.

She knew she ought to violently hate the man who was doing his best to spoil her carefully-planned scheme. True, she admired him as being the only force she had to really consider seriously in her calculations, but that would not prevent her from hating him. Wisdom told her to put him forever out of her way, for something whispered to her that the unconscious man on the bed would keep on, like an unrelenting Nemesis.

But a curious contraction stirred her heart-strings as she gazed at the strong features. What caused it she knew not, but instead of hatred against him she felt the hot blood surge into her eyes. Confused and at a loss, she turned away, not knowing why her pulses throbbed with such exquisite pain. Her tense gaze had possibly recalled the wandering consciousness of the prostrate man, for he opened his eyes and gazed vaguely about.

Tinker gave a cry and sprang forward. The deep eyes gleamed with momentary joy and relief as they recognised the lad's; they swung again and gazed steady for a moment into the strangely-softened eyes of the woman, but unconsciousness again stepped in claiming them, and they dropped as the reeling mind once more wandered.

Yvonne stumbled with a strange dizziness from the room, passing the returning Hendricks as she did so.

"Give him one of the tablets in the jar every ten minutes until he has had six," she said thickly. "He will sleep deeply, and in the morning be none the worse for his fall."

Hendricks nodded. He was surprised at her voice, which was usually so clear; but although an indulgent and kind mistress, Yvonne ruled with a stern hand, and he dared not question her. He hurried in and found the elder man bending over Blake with a cynical smile on his thin lips.

Tinker was still kneeling beside the bed, chafing Blake's wrists, and paid no attention as Yvonne's uncle spoke.

"I thought my niece the one exception among women," he drawled cynically, as Hendricks approached the bed. "But alas! I see she has wandered from the strictly safe paths."

"How do you mean, sir?" asked Hendricks.

"My boy," drawled the other, "she is falling in love with our attractive-looking friend on the bed! She doesn't know it herself yet, or it wouldn't have shown in her eyes; but she will find it out before long. I think—yes, I decidedly think— Hendricks, I should be doing a very wise thing if I took matters in my own hands and assisted our prostrate friend on his journey to the other world, but—well! I have seen my adorable niece in a few tempers, and I don't think I'll risk it. Give him the stuff as she directs, Hendricks. Perhaps she may persuade him to join us—who knows?"

He strolled from the room with the cynical smile still on his lips, and languidly drew out his cigarette-case as he finished speaking.

He had spoken in an inconsequent drawl, but his eyes hardened when he got into the passage, and his jaw set firmly as he quickened his steps and hastened to the laboratory.

Yvonne sat before the desk, her chin resting on her hand and a far-away look in her eyes.

She glanced unseeingly at her uncle as he entered, but the expression of his face drew her quickly back to the present.

"What is it?" she asked, reading the look in his eyes.

"You've made a big mistake!" he snapped, as he dropped into a chair opposite her. "It's a mistake you'll live to regret! Mark my words!"

"To what do you refer?" she asked coolly.

"Why, to this man Blake, of course. Are you so confident of your own powers that you think you can turn him loose again? If you are, I'm not; and I think you should consider me and the others in the matter. You yourself laid down the strict discipline and rules by which we should operate, and on that basis I threw in my lot with you. But what is the result—you yourself are the first one to break them."

"In what way, might I inquire, have I broken any of the rules of the circle?"

"By allowing this man to live, of course. Also keeping that boy here. You don't seem to realise that this man Blake is the cleverest detective living. He solves problems in the same way in which you create them. For Heaven's sake can't you see the risk?"

"Listen, uncle," replied Yvonne calmly. "Don't get excited. As for breaking any rules I may have made, I haven't done so. Be good enough to leave matters in my hands. I assure you, I know what I am doing. As for this man Blake— poof!"—and she snapped her fingers in disdain— "he's not half as clever as you think. Everybody weaves a halo around his head because he had been successful; but wait, he hasn't had methods like mine to combat. I haven't any intention of allowing him to go free—nor the boy, either. What I shall eventually do with them I don't know yet; possibly I will follow your suggestion, but in the meantime I propose removing them from here to the yacht, and will take them to the island. Afterwards I will decide."

"Very well," replied Graves moodily. "Of course, you do as you think best; but again I say he ought to be put aside while we have him. When will you take him to the yacht?" he continued.

"In a day or two. I'm going to London to-morrow to make another attempt to go through his desk. He must have notes, and I want to know if possible, just what Bechstein's condition is. My information led me to believe he would be forced into bankruptcy, but he is still holding on. I will dress as the boy again. It seemed to work pretty well last time," she smiled.

Meanwhile, Hendricks had been working over the unconscious Blake, whose regular breathing indicated a natural slumber.

He administered the last tablet, and after carefully locking the steel door, joined the others in the laboratory.

Tinker pulled up a chair, and with anxious eyes watched the rise and fall of Blake's chest all through the long hours of the night.

.   .   .   .

About ten the next morning a big, grey motor pulled up in Baker Street, and the driver, who descended, looked extremely like Tinker.

At any rate, the casual observer would have thought so, for he ran up the steps and quickly fitted the key to the lock, throwing open the door with a familiar air.

He hastened down the passage and into the consulting-room, but pulled up sharply as he saw the figure of a man sitting in a chair.

Before the lad had time to speak, the visitor had swung round, and the disguised Yvonne's heart jumped as she recognised Bechstein.

"Did you wish to see Mr. Blake?" ventured Yvonne, in as good an imitation of Tinker's voice as was possible.

"Yes," replied the jeweller. "I had an appointment with him this morning. But who are you—his assistant?"

"Yes," answered Yvonne, realising from his question that he had never seen Tinker, and, that if she was careful she might gain valuable information from the unexpected encounter.

"He has been unavoidably detained," she went on. "'But can I do anything for you, sir?"

Bechstein grunted.

"I don't imagine you know anything about the matter!" he snorted ungraciously. "My name's Bechstein, and Mr. Blake said he might have some progress to report this morning."

"On the contrary," said Yvonne boldly. "Mr. Blake confides fully in me. He is working on your case, Mr. Bechstein, but I am sorry to say we have nothing definite as yet. Er—it was rather urgent, wasn't it?"

"My heavens—yes," groaned Bechstein, mopping his brow. "He knows I can't hang out much longer if it isn't recovered soon. Have you any idea when he'll be back?" he asked, his face breaking into anxious lines.

"No, not exactly," replied Yvonne, dropping her lids to hide the gleam of satisfaction in her eyes, as she saw her victim squirm. "You see, he's working on it now, and won't be back until he has something definite to report. Perhaps he will be back this evening. You might ring up on the 'phone, in any event."

"All right, I will," grunted Bechstein moodily, as he rose.

Yvonne turned to the desk as the door closed behind him. She had really gained, by a fortunate accident, the information she needed, but would run through Blake's papers while she had the opportunity. Another such chance might not occur again. She had reached the desk, and was leaning over it when the bed-room door opened. Her head dropped as she looked up, but she gasped with relief as she saw the intruder was only the big hound. She would send him back to the bed-room.

Moving over to the dog, who stood gazing at her, she leaned down and patted his head.

Pedro sniffed the clothes in a curious manner. That they were Tinker's he knew, but the one who wore them he knew was not his young master. The intelligent beast worried over the master, and, lifting his head, gazed with a puzzled expression at Yvonne.

He was unable to solve the mystery, but his instinct evidently told him there was something wrong.

He resisted Yvonne's efforts to push him in the bed-room, and gently and firmly forced her back to a chair. Yvonne grew nervous as she saw the dog's persistency. She had her revolver, but dared not use it in the room. Leaning down, she laughed and patted Pedro, rising as she did so. Pedro submitted to her strokings, but when she rose he put up one big paw and pushed her back.

Yvonne realised the situation was desperate. She must do something soon to outwit the dog. If anyone came they would at once see something was wrong, and complications might arise.

Again she tried to get up; but as the dog once more pushed her back her face paled as the sound of a motor came from outside, and a moment later hurried footsteps came down the passage.

Who could it be? If it was someone who knew the real Tinker, the fact that Pedro was holding her forcibly in the chair would at once give her away

Pedro also heard the steps. With a deep bay he dashed to the door as the handle turned.

It was a slender chance, but Yvonne seized it. Jumping up, she dashed madly for the bed-room, and just managed to close the door as Pedro bounded back.

She stood panting, and looked for some way out. Voices reached her from the outer room, and as Yvonne recognised them, her eyes dilated with fear.

Feverishly she turned like a hunted animal. On came the footsteps straight towards the bed-room, and, with a sharp cry as the handle turned, she dashed for the half open window, and half rolled, half fell through it to the street.

THE ELEVENTH CHAPTER.   Blake and Tinker Escape.

YVONNE'S tablets had worked as she had prophesied, and Blake woke early the next morning feeling almost his old self. His head was still sore where he had hit it in falling, but, otherwise, he felt fairly fit.

Tinker's eyes were drooping with weariness but the tired lad forgot his weariness, as he saw Blake smile in the old rational way.

"I thought it was a dream, Tinker," he said, sitting up.

"How did I get here? Ah, yes, I remember falling! I seemed to remember seeing you afterwards, but I'm not sure. But where are we? What place is this?" he added, darting his eyes about the room as he spoke.

Tinker detailed all that had happened to him up until Blake had been carried in unconscious,

"'But how did they get you, guv'nor?" he asked, as he finished.

"It was my own fault," replied Blake savagely, as he explained to the lad how he had arrived at the Granger Farm, and what happened after. "I should have known such clever criminals would not depend on a flimsy old farmhouse for a retreat. I imagine we are in underground apartments." he went on, rising and making a tour of the room. "Yes, yes, stone walls, ceiling and floor; no windows; electrical ventilation. Very complete indeed; no hope here," he muttered, as he examined the massive steel door. "How many are there?" he asked, as he swung round.

"I don't know, guv'nor," answered Tinker, "I didn't see anyone, except the woman who brought the meals, until last night. There were two men and a woman there, but I know there is another man, because I saw him the night they brought me here."

"Ah," exclaimed Blake, nodding, "I remember now the woman— yes, I remember. Tinker, my lad! It is hopeless to try and break out of this prison; but we've got to get out some way. Things are serious— very. I begin to see things more clearly, and can now gauge the force we are up against."

"Yes, guv'nor—but how!?" inquired Tinker.

"We'll have to try strategy, that's all; and it may mean a big struggle. If there are only the two men we stand a chance, if we get them before they shoot, and, on the other hand, if there are more, or they shoot quickly, we are done for. However, that is a chance we've got to take."

The detective sank into a thoughtful silence, and Tinker waited patiently until that keen mind had devised some way out of their predicament.

"I've got it!" exclaimed Blake, breaking the silence. "Now, listen, Tinker!"

Rapidly he explained his plan, and Tinker nodded in understanding.

"It's risky," wound up Blake; "but it's the only way. If one of us gets through, he mustn't wait for the other, but must go as quickly as possible for help."

They shook hands silently, and Blake again lay down on the bed while Tinker prepared to carry out the scheme.

Blake closed his eyes in apparent unconsciousness while Tinker raised an unearthly din by banging at the steel door with a heavy, oaken stool.

Through the stone passage reverberated the noise, and a few moments later the slide was pushed open, Graves's face appeared in the opening, anger written on his countenance.

"Here what the—" he began; but Tinker cut him short.

"Quick!" he cried. "The guv'nor is not breathing like he was last night! There's been a big change!"

All of which was strictly true, but not in the way Graves thought. "Come and see what is the matter, please!"

"Oh, all right!" snapped the man. "I'll be back presently!"

He returned in a few moments with Hendricks, who carried the blue jar of tablets, and impatiently threw open the door.

"This man Blake is a nuisance," muttered Graves, as he walked over to the bed. "My advice should have been taken in the first place."

Neither of the men noticed Tinker walking quietly behind, still carrying the heavy, oaken stool, and still grumbling. Graves leaned over the bed.

He gave a startled cry as the apparently unconscious man seemed suddenly to turn into a galvanic battery.

Up shot his arm like a bar of iron, gripping unerringly at Graves's throat. Quickly Blake's body followed his arm, and, as the other gathered his wits together they gripped in deadly silence. Hendricks' jaw had dropped in astonishment at the sudden attack; but almost before Blake had seized Graves, Hendricks had instinctively turned.

He was just in time, for Tinker was leaping for him, the oaken stool upraised ready to strike.

Without a moment's hesitation Hendricks hurled the heavy blue jar at Tinker. Had it hit the lad it would have killed him at once; but glancing off the stool, it caught him in the side of the head. He staggered with the shock, and, as Hendricks leaped forward, Tinker found it was too close quarters to use the stool.

Dropping it, he grappled as the other reached him, and down they went, rolling over and over in the struggle until they brought up with a jerk against the other struggling pair.

Silently the quartet fought. Graves was a powerful man; but Blake's muscles were like steel springs, and it was evident that the detective was slowly overpowering his antagonist. But with the other two fortune lay the other way.

A sailor's life had made Hendricks accustomed to fighting, and he was a much more powerful man than the lad. Although Tinker fought gamely, he was still dizzy from the effects of the blow from the jar, and he gasped as he felt himself slowly giving in.

The struggle still hung in the balance. If Blake overpowered his man before Hendricks subdued Tinker, he could go to Tinker's assistance, and the day was theirs.

On the other hand, if Hendricks succeeded in beating Tinker before Graves gave in he could attack Blake, and thus win the day. All four combatants realised this, and none more so than Tinker, who, knowing he must inevitably go under, devoted all his remaining strength toward retaining his senses, and keeping Hendricks occupied until Blake could come. Graves was doing the same on his part, and the grim race went on as the panting men struggled for the mastery.

But hard as he fought, Tinker felt the iron grip tightening on his throat. His eyes blurred as he choked. Valiantly he gave one more supreme effort; but the ever-tightening grip did not relax. Slowly his head dropped; everything reeled madly around; his eyes closed, and he was dimly aware of a crushing weight falling on him as he sank into unconsciousness.

That weight which Tinker vaguely thought was his death, was in reality Hendricks crashing down, as Blake, having overcome Graves, leaped to Tinker's assistance, Hendricks released his hold on Tinker's throat, and turned and grappled with Blake: but the latter had a steel-like grip of the sailor's throat, and, as the detective planted his knee in the small of Hendricks' back, he sank with a fierce cry of pain.

Blake was taking no chances, and, before attending unconscious Tinker, he securely bound and gagged and Hendricks, ripping up the sheets for his purpose.

After being satisfied that they were now incapable of mischief, he turned to Tinker, and soon had the lad on his feet.

"Crikey, guv'nor, that was a close one!" said the lad, ruefully rubbing his neck. "I thought he had me—certain."

"He nearly did," laughed the still panting Blake, "But come, we have no time to waste! Others may arrive soon, and Heaven knows how long it may take us to get out of this place!"

"What will you do with these two?" asked Tinker.

"We'll leave them here for the present, and lock them in. If, as I think, the steel door locks with a secret combination, the serving woman won't know what it is, and, as they are well gagged, they can't tell her. You don't look very presentable in those clothes," he smiled grimly; "but I hope to be able to personally secure your own ere long. We have still got the chief one to get yet, and I think I can guess where that one is, since she isn't here. What a wonderful woman!" he muttered to himself. "And what a pity!"

As Blake had thought, the steel door was worked by a combination. Hastily examining it he closed the door, and swung it round.

"That will hold them until we come back," he said, as he changed the combination to a different cipher.

The detective made a rapid survey of the different rooms as they made their way down the passage, and his eyes were filled with admiration when they reached the stairs leading up to the stone exit.

"Marvellous!" he muttered. "And to think she has conceived all this without my being aware of her existence! What a brain—what thoroughness! Truly, my unknown friend, you give the chase a decided zest!"

A short examination by Blake discovered the button which released the stone door. He pressed it, and located the outer one before allowing the big stone to swing to.

Making for the door he led the way over the open into the woods, and kept on across country at a rapid pace until Colby was reached.

It was the work of a few moments to secure the big grey car and start the engine.

Tinker refrained from speaking as Blake sent the machine forward at a bound, for he knew the detective's moods too well to break in on his line of thought when the deep eyes held the look they did at present.

Blake certainly never drove more recklessly than he did on that journey, to London.

Through villages he dashed, utterly indifferent to speed laws or the indignant remarks the outraged farmers shouted after him.

Turning into Baker Street, Tinker expected to see him slow up, but the sight of another grey car outside his apartments only spurred him on. He did not slacken speed until within a short distance of the door, and, sharply throwing out the clutch, he put on the brake, skidding wildly into the kerb and stopping a bare inch from the other car.

Without a word he dashed out and up the steps, followed by Tinker.

Down the passage went the hurried steps, and, for once disregarding Pedro's demonstrations, he headed for the bed-room door, the handle of which his keen eyes had seen move as he entered the Consuiting-room.

"Quick, Tinker; follow me!" cried Blake, as he opened the bed-room door and saw a figure disappear through the window.

On he rushed, following the fugitive through the window, with Tinker and Pedro tumbling after him.

Yvonne, for she was the fugitive, dashed on, and gained her car, the engine of which was still running. She swung the wheel and started to move as Blake gained the side walk and came on in pursuit.

"Stop!" he cried, pulling out a revolver and levelling it; but Yvonne leaned low as the car gained speed. Swinging it straight into the road, she sat up and pulled out her own revolver.

Blake was firing low in order to try and hit the tyres, and Yvonne could hear the lead pattering on the machine. Swinging around, she took careful aim, and through luck or cleverness, her bullet reached her mark in one of Blake's tyres.

With a muttered exclamation Blake dashed to his car and began to rapidly unbuckle his spare wheel. Tinker was filled with amazement at the astonishing reproduction of himself in the other car, but, as he hastened to assist Blake, he refrained from asking questions when he saw the detective's jaw, as, for the second time in twenty-four hours, a silvery, mocking laugh floated back.

THE TWELFTH CHAPTER. Blake and Tinker Again Prisoners.

BLAKE had spent a small fortune in having a motor built according to his own designs, and many times had the wisdom of his action been proved, but never more so than at the present time, for no ordinary car could have withstood the racking pace at which the detective started in pursuit.

As the new wheel had been clamped home, he turned and ordered Pedro back to watch the house, and jumped, without further word, for the wheel, leaving Tinker to get aboard as best he could. Into the tonneau tumbled the lad, and when his tangled legs had separated, climbed over the seat and sat beside Blake.

For perhaps the first time the lad realised that they were on no ordinary chase.

He had never remembered seeing quite such a steely look in Blake's eyes before.

Back over the road which they had travelled a little earlier went the big car.

Once again the villagers gazed after the flying monster with astonishment and anger, but Blake was indifferent to everything but one idea.

The slender thread which he had followed had developed into a strong cord with amazing rapidity, and his sole object was to run to earth the mysterious power which had flouted him several times since he had taken the case. He was not accustomed to such things, and the fact that he felt confident it was a woman's brain which had devised such baffling methods made matters worse.

But even in his tense condition he smiled in grim admiration. His opponent was worthy of his greatest skill, and never before had Blake played the game with greater zest. The boldness of snapping her fingers at him by returning the ten-pound note had put Blake on his mettle, but those two silvery, mocking laughs had gone deep. Nothing now would make him stop until he had the author of them under his hand.

It was early afternoon when they pounded through Colby, and Blake kept on, without stopping, toward the Granger Farm.

They were fully a mile from the road which led up to it, when Blake gave a smothered exclamation as a grey motor turned out of it into the main road. It contained three occupants, and Blake knew Graves and Hendrick had been released. They had evidently caught sight of Blake, for they looked back steadily for a moment.

If the leading car had been an ordinary motor, Blake would have felt easy about overtaking it; but he had been only a few moments clamping on the new wheel, and the fact that it had reached the farm so quickly showed that it must be of high power.

If it was possible for his own car to go any faster, it did so, and, outside of Brooklands, probably there never was such a race between two powerful motors as took place that day between the two grey cars.

Through the afternoon that race kept on. Both drivers were giving their cars all they could stand, and it said much for the equality of both machines when three hours left them almost as they had started.

Blake had gained a trifle, but only a trifle. He could have perhaps gone a little faster, but man and machine, through constant association, had become almost one, and the detective knew any more strain on this finely-tuned engine would send it flying to pieces in all directions.

Tinker sat in silent intensity through that long chase, and not until dusk shut in did he move.

Reaching down, he pressed the button which lit the brilliant road lamps, and a gleam ahead told them the others had done likewise.

Then he refilled the petrol tank, which was under the seat.

As the darkness fell the houses grew scarcer, the country wilder, and a salt tang told them they were near the sea.

Another hour passed before the sea appeared, but when it did it met them with a rush.

Over the brow of a hill raced both cars, and as they did so, below them appeared a small bay. Close in shore lay a brilliantly-lighted yacht, and, on drawing nearer, Blake saw that it was moored to a tiny wharf.

A sudden stop ahead brought Blake up with a rush beside the leading car. Quickly throwing on the brakes, he leaped out, followed by Tinker.

He saw the reason of the stop as he drew near, for one of the tyres had a gaping hole in its flattened surface.

Both Blake and Tinker knew they must act quickly if they were to secure their quarry, for the sound of shots would bring assistance from the yacht to their enemy.

"Shoot to hit!" jerked out Blake, as he levelled his own revolver and fired. A cry rang out; Hendricks dropped. Tinker fired, and a crash told them his bullet had gone wide, hitting the wind shield. But Graves and Yvonne were now firing rapidly. Yvonne had secured the revolver with a silencer attached, and its bullets whined past in sinister silence.

"Catch her arms and hold her!" cried Blake, as he dashed forward with bent head.

Tinker did as he was bid, but Yvonne was too elusive for him. Tinker had secured many women since he had been with Blake, but never one like this, and he gasped as his hands clutched the empty air.

Once again that maddening laugh rang out, and Blake sprang with extraordinary savageness at the still shooting Graves as he heard it.

Graves had had quite enough experience of Blake's powers as a fighter at the farm, but the detective came with such a rush that he was forced to drop his revolver and grapple. As man to man, the result of that fight was a foregone conclusion. Yvonne dared not shoot, if she could, for fear of hitting her uncle, and now it was impossible, for Tinker had succeeded in gripping her arms.

Blake sank his fingers into his antagonist's throat and pressed them deep with a savage grip. He intended wasting no time in subduing Graves, and he was on a fair way to succeed, when Hendricks, who, up to now, had lain quiet where he had fallen, stumbled to his knees. Tinker gave a cry of warning as the sailor picked up his revolver and gained his feet, but it was no avail. As Blake turned to meet the new danger, Hendricks struck, and the detective dropped like a stone.

Tinker left Yvonne, and dashed forward, but he was soon overpowered and bound.

The two prisoners were packed into the tonneau of Blake's car, and Yvonne drove it at a slow pace down to the wharf.

As they were carried aboard, Tinker recognised the man who had conducted him to his prison at the farm. Several others, dressed in seamen's uniforms, stood around, but he had no time to see anything else. They were quickly carried down a companion-way and through a brilliantly-lighted saloon to the door of a cabin.

One of the uniformed sailors threw this open, and the captives were tossed unceremoniously into the bunks.

Blake appeared still unconscious, but Tinker lay back gloomily as the door closed and the lock clicked.

Outside in the luxurious saloon, Yvonne leaned against the table while Hendricks' wound was attended to.

When it had been bound up and his arm strapped to his side—for it was in the shoulder—two of the sailors assisted him to his cabin.

Captain Vaughan had retired to the bridge to get the yacht under way, and Yvonne and her uncle were left alone in the saloon.

"Well," drawled Graves, "I trust you are satisfied? If you had done as I wished this would never have happened. It's the closest shave I ever saw, and if Hendricks hadn't come just in time we would all have been prisoners in the tonneau of this confounded Blake's car."

"I had no chance to express my opinion of your intelligence when you told me in the car how he escaped." replied Yvonne icily. "But I will do so now. You and Hendricks must be about as clever as a piece of wood. Oh, you babies, to be taken in as you were'"

"You would have been yourself!" snapped Graves sulkily.

"You know better than that, uncle," replied Yvonne. "Heavens, what madness to go in as you did! You who held him up as such a wizard, to trust yourself that way. Did you forget who he was? Didn't you know if there was one chance escape, Sexton Blake would seize it as soon as he awoke? You see now that he did. But I shall take it upon myself this time to see that he doesn't get another chance."

"What do you propose doing?" inquired Graves.

"I'm going to offer him the chance of joining us. With him we could achieve anything. If he refuses—well, he'll have to go. He's too dangerous to be free!"

"You'd better marry him," drawled Graves, his old manner returning. "You'd make a nice king and queen. I'd certainly—"

"Stop?" exclaimed Yvonne, going deathly pale. "Don't take a liberty, uncle! I won't permit it!"

Graves flushed as she spoke; for although he was older, and her uncle as well, he stood in awe of Yvonne, as did all who surrounded her. She dominated her associates by sheer force of character, and her word was never questioned.

"Well, don't get wild," replied Graves, "I didn't mean anything."

"Very well; but kindly remember not to make such a remark again. And now leave me, please," she added wearily. "Send two men to bring Sexton Blake here, and don't allow anyone to disturb me until I have finished."

Graves departed to do her bidding, and Yvonne sank into a deep chair and awaited her prisoner's arrival.

THE THIRTEENTH CHAPTER.   Yvonne's Offer to Blake—
The End.

TINKER had fallen into a deep sleep, and did not hear the cabin door open to admit the two sailors who had been sent for Blake.

They carried the still unconscious detective outside, and entered the saloon.

He came round under the invigorating effect of some raw spirit, and blinked around dazedly as the brilliant lights hit his eyes. His hands were tied behind him, but otherwise he was free to move. He leaned against the table as the sailors took their departure, and not until then did he see the woman in the chair.

Long and silently did those two look at one another.

All about them was the magnificent saloon, its further corners softened by shaded lights. Only over the gleaming white of the silver-covered tablecloth did the lights shine with unrestrained brilliancy. The beautiful oak and black palm woodwork gleamed somberly amongst the rich upholstering, and underfoot the deep carpet increased the restful atmosphere of the saloon.

The beautiful, bronze-haired woman, sitting in the deep chair was a fitting decoration to its harmony, and the lack of a single jarring note reflected credit on the woman, who had designed it.

Overhead sounded the occasional sound of feet as the sailors obeyed the commands of the captain, but both occupants of that deep-toned saloon were too intent on the coming test of wits to hear.

Yvonne's eyes dropped as she rose and walked toward the detective.

Stopping in front of him, and placing her hands behind her back, she smiled; and Blake, as he looked into her eyes, was compelled to smile in return.

"I must congratulate you," he said, bowing. "You have succeeded, so far, most admirably."

"Why the emphasis on the 'so far'?" she smiled back.

"Do you consider the game played out yet?" inquired Blake, also smiling.

"Not quite," she replied. "But I'm afraid you must confess the next move lies with me, Mr. Blake."

"At the present moment I must confess it does. But one never knows when the tide may turn." answered Blake.

Had she seen his hands stealthily reach out behind him and pull towards him one of the shining knives which lay on the table in anticipation of the coming meal, she would have seen that, as usual, he had seized the first opportunity of turning the tide.

"I'm afraid there is little chance of it turning this time." she replied saucily. "But I wish to make a serious proposition to you. Mr. Blake."

Blake glanced in puzzlement, as Yvonne half turned away, her face changing from white to red, and back to white again. He kept silent, however, and awaited her reply, although his hands were all the time cautiously working as industriously as his bonds would allow.

Again Yvonne began to speak, and her voice was strangely unsteady for one of her assurance.

"I—I—" she began hesitatingly. "Oh, it is very hard to say!" she went on hurriedly. "But, believe me, I have never before talked to any man, or permitted any man to talk to me in such a way. But you must realise that now I have you in my power I cannot permit you to go free and always menace my plans."

Blake's look of wonderment deepened as she spoke, for he had no idea of what was to follow.

"You must be put out of the way!" continued Yvonne, her head still averted. "But there's one alternative."

"What's that?" asked Blake quietly, as she paused.

"It is that you join us—join us in every sense of the word! Wait, hear me out!" she cried, raising her hand as Blake started to reply. "They had not erred in their estimate of your cleverness," she continued; "but I am clever, too. I have already made a large fortune, but with you we could have anything we wished, and who would say 'Nay'? I am lonely! Oh, can't you understand?"

Yvonne turned away in shy embarrassment. Blake forgot the criminal, and saw only the lovely girl who had offered herself to him.

"I am sorry," he said gently, "but it is impossible! My duty lies in stamping out crime, not promoting it. And my wife—if I ever have one—must not be on the side of crime."

Yvonne swung round sharply as Blake spoke the last sentence. The blood departed from her face, leaving, it like marble. Her wonderful eyes gleamed like flashing points, her breast heaved with pent-up emotion.

"You—you—I hate you!" she said, in a voice of deadly calm.

"Do you know what you have done? I have humbled myself! I a woman of birth, wealth, brains, humbled myself to you, and you throw my gift back in my face! For that, if even for nothing else, you will die!"

Blake stood like a carven piece of granite as she spoke intensely. It was an uncomfortable position, but he deemed silence the wiser plan; and besides, he wasn't so sure about being put aside so easily as he felt the cords drop from his hands.

Yvonne approached nearer. Every moment she seemed to be getting angrier at the blow her pride had received. Finally verbal chastisement failed to satisfy her, and she leaned forward, lifting her hand to strike the detective. Through the air swished the white, jewelled arm, but it never reached its mark, for an arm of steel shot out and grasped the white wrist, and before the astounded Yvonne could cry out Blake's other hand covered her mouth as she struggled in his arms.

"Be quiet'!" he breathed. "I've got the whip-hand, and I mean to use it! You claim to have brains; if so, you must use them. You are a woman, and I don't want to use force. Pass me the word you will not give the alarm, and I will release you?"

"I promise!" she nodded; and Blake, knowing she would keep her word, released her.

"That's better!" he exclaimed, as she dropped into the chair. "Now we can talk comfortably. Firstly, by the way, I haven't the honour of knowing your name. Permit me to formally introduce myself although it seems unnecessary, as you already know my name—Sexton Blake, mademoiselle, at your service." smiled Blake bowing.

"Charmed!" replied Yvonne rising, and returning the bow with mock politeness. "Mademoiselle Yvonne is honoured!"

"Am I not to know the other name as well?" asked Blake.

"Not yet!" .she replied maliciously.

"Well, that's too bad," he went on again, smiling, "It forces me to the exertion of finding it out."

"And I believe you will!" cut in Yvonne viciously.

"Well, we will let it pass. As I said, firstly Mademoiselle Yvonne, I arrest you, in the name of the King, for the robbery, from a Bond Street jewellery establishment, of a valuable pearl necklace!" and he added, in mock seriousness "Let me warn you, that anything you say may be used against you!"

"Thank you!" replied Yvonne, "But how do you propose to take me to prison?"

"Easiest thing in the world," answered Blake. "You'll see when the time comes!" he added, dropping his bantering tone.

"Tell me, please, how did you trace me?" asked Yvonne.

"It would be very foolish for me to tell you my methods," laughed Blake, "You might turn detective when you get out of this and take all my clients away."

"I cannot see where I left, any tracks," mused Yvonne.

"You didn't; at least, none that could possibly be eliminated." broke in Blake.

Silence reigned for some moments.

Yvonne was sunk in pensive thought, while Blake's mind worked rapidly, devising some plan to free Tinker and get past the sailors with his prisoner. A plan had just occurred to him when Yvonne spoke again.

"I wonder if you'd care to hear why I took up this profession?" she asked.

"I would, indeed," replied Blake; "if it won't take, too long."

"It won't. I'll be brief."

Rapidly she ran over the story of the mine swindle which had killed her mother, and sent her into the world, her heart seething with the thoughts of revenge.

Blake listened silently as she unfolded the story, and his lips shut in a straight line as she reached the time when she landed in England prepared for her work.

"I had kept track of Vineburg all these years," she went on. "and when he left Australia after a crooked deal on the race-track, I followed him. He took the name of Bechstein, and with the money he had made bought jewelry establishment in Bond Street. For five years I watched him while I perfected my training, and when I was ready to strike, I struck. I took him first because he was the chief mover in the deal."

"I'm astounded at your story!" remarked Blake. "And I believe it. Bechstein came to me, and asked me to take up the case. Naturally, I did so; but had I known his full history, I would not have done so. But having started off on the case, I must finish it. You have done wrong, and have broken the law. I am not a preacher," he smiled; "but it is not for each man to take the law in his own hands. If that were the case, anarchy and chaos would reign. I don't doubt that Bechstein has done you a great wrong; but if he kept within man's law—well, rest assured he will one day be fully punished. However, after what you tell me, I will not arrest you. The actual crime part is for Scotland Yard to take up. I will not start them on the case; but if Bechstein does, I must give evidence. That is all I can promise you. What I must insist upon, however, is the return of the necklace. That I insist on, for I cannot permit myself to enter the word failure in my index."

"What if I refuse?" asked Yvonne, looking up.

"You won't," answered Blake quietly. "But if you did, I'd have to re-arrest you, and take you with me."

"Do you realise that as soon as some supplies arrive, the yacht will at once put out to sea?"

"That makes no difference. I will take you back, nevertheless."

"I believe you would," she muttered softly.

"We'll call a truce, Mr. Blake," she added, rising, "I'll return you the pearls, and for to-night we will be friends."

"With pleasure," smiled Blake. "But I must ask you to pledge your word you will communicate with no one while you go to fetch the pearls."

"Would you take my word for that?" she asked curiously.

"Yes; in your case."

Yvonne departed, and returned shortly, with the magnificent string of gems.

"Here they are," she laughed.

"Thank you!" answered Blake, as Yvonne moved to the table, and poured out some wine.

"To our next meeting!" she flashed, lifting her glass, Blake took the challenge, and drank the toast.

Five minutes later, with the released Tinker following, he strode through the hostile stares of astonishment of Yvonne's associates, and passed over the side.

He pulled up the motor at the top of the hill, and gazed back.

Below the brilliantly-lighted yacht was backing slowly from the tiny pier. Overhead the stars shone in pale splendour, and all around the trees banked in a sombre background.

"Poor little girl!" he muttered, as the yacht's head came round. "What a pity! What a brilliant mind, and what a detective she would make! To our next meeting—eh?" he breathed softly. "It promises well, mademoiselle." And, strangely stirred, Blake threw in the clutch; and sent the car bounding toward London.

"Tell me, guv'nor," asked Tinker, as they sat before the fire several hours later, "how did you pick up the trail of the pearls. I've puzzled over the points you told me, but I couldn't make anything of it."

"You hardly could." laughed Blake. "It was a case strictly out of the normal; but it proves what I have always contended—that the present-day investigator of crime must keep ahead in every line of science. But I'll show you how I followed it up.

"You remember," went on the detective, puffing thoughtfully at his pipe, "how I told you the case narrowed down— either Bechstein, or one other thing?"

Tinker nodded, and Blake continued:

"Well, I had to eliminate Bechstein from the matter, and only the other thing remained. You remember only three people had examined the necklace. It stood to reason that some time must be spent if designs were to be prepared for a substitute. Everything pointed to that being an impossibility. How then could a design have been obtained? you ask.

"Only one way is known which will give an instantaneous reproduction of an article, and that is photography. But ordinary photography would not do, and, besides, a camera would be too bulky. The next point was—what kind of photography would do? Only one, and that was so new to science as to be still in the experimental stage. It was hardly probable that any criminal would know enough, and adopt it. Still, after hours of deduction, everything pointed to that.

"True, it was a weak thread to work on, but in the absence of any other it had to be utilised. Consequently, working on that hypothesis when, if so, had the necklace been photographed? As each of the three had only visited Bechstein's once it was obvious that two of the three had been working in collusion—one to take the embossed photograph, and one to make the exchange.

"Sir George Wallington was beyond suspicion. Only the other two remained, and it was necessary to search every detail of their visit.

"Bechstein's office, where the necklace was viewed, is fairly dark, and for a detailed photograph, an artificial light must be used. The camera, in order to be invisible, and yet handy for use, must be secreted in a place which would hide it, and yet bring it freely into play. Bechstein accidentally noticed what he thought was a flash of sun on the gold head of the supposed American's walking-stick. I read a different meaning. What better place could be devised for the purpose than the handle of a walking-stick?

"In it could be placed a small camera suitable for embossed photography made specially for the purpose. The sudden flash was the artificial light used for the purpose. That, naturally, was a risk, but not as great a risk as one would think, for, unless one was looking straight at it, the flash would be over so soon that it would be hard to locate it exactly. And, of course, there are now several different methods of applying a flash without the attendant smoke of the old powders, which would be out of the question in a case of this kind."

Tinker's eyes glistened with excitement as Blake paused to relight his pipe.

"Then," continued the detective, "we have in support, the fact that the man was the second caller. Then came the woman. Did she get an opportunity to make the exchange while there? Yes, if she were clever enough; for to allay any suspicion she went to the trouble of purchasing a fairly expensive necklace, and while the jeweller turned his back to get a box for it, if she were quick, and had the nerve, she could do it. And you have seen whether she has the nerve or not," he added grimly.

"The next step was to trace the identity of both man and woman. There I was at a loss. The nun's visit puzzled me, and I did not connect it with the case at first. I thought she might be a masquerading swindler; but when you went in pursuit and did not return, and later in the evening I found the ten-pound note under the door, I knew I had been watched, and that some powerful, unknown force was working against me.

"What had been puzzling me about the embossed photograph of the necklace was how it could be enlarged to the exact scale of the object photographed. I had been working on this same line myself, but as yet had discovered no method.

"In a photographic journal I came across a most exhaustive article on this point, and saw that it was entirely possible. Could there be any connection? Hardly. Still, it must be followed up. I told you of my interview with the editor, and how the trail led me to Barnesley in Surrey. From that point, you know the rest, and can see the line I followed. But we should not have fared nearly so well, and the chase would have lasted much longer if Pedro hadn't taken a hand."

The big hound raised his head as Blake spoke his name, and rising, struck his cold muzzle against the detective's knee.

"Yes," he went on, "it was evident to me that Pedro had been keeping her here by force, for otherwise, he would not have bayed as he did."

"I wish I had my clothes back," remarked Tinker.

"You'll get them," laughed Blake. "Mademoiselle Yvonne promised to send them, and she'll keep her word."

"Bechstein will be glad to get his pearls back, won't he, guv'nor?" continued Tinker.

"Yes. I imagine he will." replied Blake curtly, for he had not told Tinker what Yvonne had confided to him. "I see he has been here to-night," he added: "I noticed his card on the desk as I came in. He probably came to inquire what progress we had made. And now, my lad, let's to bed. We will call on Bechstein early in the morning, and give him the pearls."

Rising, they turned out the lights, and Tinker did not hear the muttered remark which Blake made as he passed into his room. Had he done so, he would have wondered as to its meaning, for it was:

"To our next meeting."

But Bechstein was not to receive the pearls. The next morning when Blake and Tinker arrived they found a curious crowd about the door, and, on forcing his way through, Blake was informed by a policeman that Mr. Bechstein had shot himself in the night, and from a short note which he had left they had gathered that it had been caused by financial worries.

Blake and Tinker turned away, and left the place to the police.

Blake's idea, which happened to be correct, was that Bechstein had called to see if anything had been discovered about the necklace, and, not finding Blake at home, had given up hope. Had he waited, as Blake had told him to do until the banks opened the next day, which was Bechstein's final day of grace, he would have weathered the storm, for Blake and Tinker had arrived at Bond Street long before the time.

But Fate had decreed otherwise, and by Bechstein's own hand had Yvonne been revenged.

THE END.
[35100 WORDS, NOVELETTE]

I know that everybody has enjoyed this yarn to the full, so *the announcement that there will be another YVONNE v. SEXTON BLAKE yarn soon, will be hailed with delight and approval. The title* of *the next Yvonne yarn will be: WHEN GREEK MEETS GREEK,* or *THE BULLION THIEVES."*
The Skipper.

Also in this issue were 'A Word from The Skipper' and one part of the serial 'Charlie Gordon's Schooldays'.

www.ingramcontent.com/pod-product-compliance
Lightning Source LLC
Chambersburg PA
CBHW031852170626
46807CB00004B/1690